I0682963

Pluto Dreams
of Persephone

Kevin O. Shoemaker

This is a work of fiction.
All the characters and events portrayed in this novel are either
fictitious or are used fictitiously.

Pluto Dreams of Persephone
Copyright © 2015 by Kevin O. Shoemaker

This book is printed on acid free paper

A Shoemaker Labs Book
Indian Harbour Beach, Florida
e-mail: Shoemakerlabs@gmail.com

ISBN-13: 978-0-9815092-7-3
ISBN-10: 0-9815092-7-4

Registered with the Library of Congress

Interior Layout & Design by Integrative Ink

First edition October, 2015
Printed in the United States of America

This book is dedicated to the Scientists and Engineers who designed, tested, flew and interpreted the data sent from the New Horizons space probe. Led by Alan Stern, this group of highly talented individuals came together to closely explore and thus completely re-write our understanding of our ninth planet, Pluto.

Acknowledgment

I would like to sincerely thank Jack Shoemaker for his editing and comments. Also, I would like to thank my friends Peg, Ed, Joy and Savanna for their editing and comments. Finally, I would like to thank my daughter Leah and son Stephen, for their encouragement and patience.

INTRODUCTION

Before I begin, I have to tell all of you that I cannot verify that these stories have or have not really transpired. I am restricted by the level of security clearance I hold to validate or acknowledge any particular details without first establishing a need to know basis. As with the highest clearances, the holder of what we call "the ticket" can only know and work with a portion of the complete story. Therefore I cannot confirm or deny any of the details of the following scenarios.

This book is also written in honor of the New Horizons spacecraft which at this very moment is closing in on Pluto. Almost every day new images are being received of the planet and its moons that are better than the last. The probe is moving very quickly and will only be in the system for a few hours. It is now re-writing history with every data packet it sends back to Earth.

I had the distinct pleasure of working with several of the planetary scientists from Southwest Research in Boulder, Colorado, doing stellar occultation measurements in some of the best world class observatories on Earth. It was a thrill to work with such talented people and a thrill to use these great discovery machines. From our measurement we discovered details about Pluto's atmosphere that will be compared to those measured by the probe during the close encounter of July 14, 2015.

A constant theme in this book is....if you want to experience the future, you need to invent it.

Please enjoy the book as much as I enjoyed writing it and if you have any comments or questions, I can be reached at shoemakerlabs@gmail.com

Thank you,

Kevin O. Shoemaker
Indian Harbour Beach, Florida
Dublin, Ireland
October 2015

TABLE OF CONTENTS

Introduction vii

Pluto and Persephone 1

Nina 26

What Future Hath we Wrought? 47

Tele-presence on another world.... 62

The Mayan Poles 71

Mars Hibernation 97

Time Travel..... 124

Clones Now 133

Grace and Starden 167

The Magician 194

Mumtaz Mahal 201

Perfect Memory 215

Notable Quotes 231

About the Author 233

PLUTO AND PERSEPHONE

"Wonder is the beginning of Wisdom." – *Greek Proverb*

It was three in the morning; he was wide awake and ready to start the journey. No reason to stay in bed and stare at the ceiling-too much adrenaline was coursing through his veins. It was time. He grabbed his backpack, the last vestige of personal property in the hotel room. Slinging it over his shoulder he approached the door, seeing light leaking in from the streetlamp surrounded by a cloud of bugs. The door shut succinctly and he strode to his van in that quiet night.

It had been an eventful month. His wife had let him know he could move away, his new job took him into the depths of top secret spacecraft design and he had helped discover life in the Universe. Not to keep things boring, he had also obtained his scuba diving certificate and was now flying twin engine aircraft from a local airport. Life abundant within a sphere of hollowness. Why must his life be incomplete? It's not like he did not deserve it, but he felt that it was not to be, at least not now.

The van started easily, he checked the gauges and quickly commanded the transmission to back him out of this cheap hotel car space then onto the road home and away from the thin life. Traffic was light as expected and the lights were in his favor tonight, giving him the impression that the Universe confirmed that this was the right thing to do. Within a few minutes he turned towards the highway, where the highest speeds and quickest arrival would be possible. On the way, he looked for coffee, but was realistic about the prospects as any 3 am coffee would have been started in a 10 pm pot. He looked for this half-heartedly knowing that within a few hours better coffee would appear down the road somewhere.

Fifteen minutes later the right blinker was engaged, the van redirected and acceleration commenced to engage the highway with its professionals and dunces. Safe though it may be, no one is to be trusted here as most people know that when you discuss accidents, cars are by far the greatest offenders. The best thing to do is pay attention, engage the cruise control and periodically enjoy the scenery. It was also a good habit to look for an achievable goal in terms of range, pick a city that could have decent hotels and food plus the possibility of locating a beer or two to calm the frayed nerves from the day's drive.

Sitting back in the seat now, keeping track of the cars and trucks in front and in back of him, he could now think about what had transpired recently. He hoped up front that things would work out with his wife as she ultimately knew that there was no-one better for her. He had no illusions about his adoration and that would give him the energy to complete the work to heal the relationship. He had not wandered in his love for her, never considered another woman for companionship or lust and never intentionally hurt her for any reason. 'Unintentionally' however is where root of the problem was, as individuals have individual thoughts and actions and he was a particularly individual person. His mind moved from science to engineering to flying to friends to family to future in a sometimes chaotic fashion, leaving those with more organized thought processes confused. There was never any mal-intent, just nonstop mental activity. Once, a close friend accused him of thinking continuously, a concept he thought was universal, not ever having experienced mental silence. He discovered later that it might not be the norm. He surmised after this discovery that this reality could be dealt with by always keeping intellectually active; memory would at times lapse but the process would continue. The experiences had all been recorded and sometimes with effort, could be retrieved. Others could remember every day of their life or all of what they had learned, but even they had periodic silence. Marshall Daedalus was not so lucky, or unlucky depending on your perspective.

The road was straight, black and covered in cool air as the van traveled northwest towards home. Most drivers this time of night were civil; the drunks had fallen asleep, been arrested or crashed by now. The professionals were moving their big rigs authoritatively and the remaining drivers seemed to have purpose tonight. Some stars were visible and the setting planets gave a reference to time and direction.

Marshall expected the phone calls to start early as the knowledge and acceptance of the discovery of life settled into the scientific community. The public would know soon and this would start an avalanche of discussions and controversy. The religious would have to make adjustments, the scientists would have to confirm and the philosophers would have to raise their heads to look up into a new reality.

It had been pretty straight forward: his intuitions and calculations led him to write a proposal to use a new telescope called ALMA in northern Chile. He had taken a left turn when most every other scientist had taken a right. They looked for signals revealing intelligent communications. He looked for the subtle signatures of life in general. For instance, Methane, water, CO^2 and a host of others. He realized a long time ago that water and life were always closely connected and that speculation about non-water-based life required quite a few assumptions, one being that it would have to be very rare. Another realization he had was that life is easy to start and hard to eliminate. It had been found thousands of feet below the surface of the Earth, at the very lowest points in the oceans, in clouds and on meteors. Given enough time, life can find a way to exist and multiply in most any environment within reason. Within reason meant within areas around stars known as the "Goldilocks Zone," which were neither too hot nor too cold. The vast majority of stars have planets, in fact it was difficult to find ones without planets. They came in all sizes and distances with many near the size of Earth and within the habitable zone. Most stars were stable just like ours and soon it became apparent that life could very well be thriving on many planets. The numbers were in the many thousands for just the local community alone. Extrapolation of the true numbers of habitable planets in our Milky Way alone rose quickly into the many billions.

Now it was time, and Marshall had been the one to think of it first. His proposal won enough funding to keep him at the radio telescope for several weeks. During this time he spent most of it in the control room, suggesting new targets and new frequency bands. The bands were the areas where chemicals produced their "radio" signature, much like looking at all of the FM signals across the dial in picture form. They looked like a series of spikes coming out the ground from the low end to the high end of the prescribed band. Each spike represented a different station just as the chemical signatures he was looking for. The spikes in this case represented individual chemical elements or compounds. These were predicable because years before his observations, laboratory experiments showed the spectral fingerprints of thousands of chemicals and mixtures of chemicals. These had been derived by mathematical formulas by some very clever chemists. For instance, Hydrogen, the most abundant element in the Universe, resonated at 1,420 MHz which was just below the frequency that GPS satellites transmitted on. Scientists in England many years ago had assembled a simple radio telescope which had verified hydrogen's place in the heavens. They found it in huge quantities in the Milky Way and had been able to observe its motions and how it interacted with the stars. Years later, hundreds and then thousands of other signatures had been observed, allowing the radio astronomers to "dial in" the chemical of interest and map it anywhere in the Universe. They found huge quantities of water this way, then CO^2 followed by many of the other chemicals produced by chemical reactions. Marshall had realized that on Earth, life produces signatures of its existence. In fact a satellite was sent into space (for another mission) and when it passed the Earth after a round about trek by other planets, was asked to observe the third planet and determine if there was life on it. It proclaimed that there was, and from this work as well as the building of the most powerful millimeter wave radio telescope, he as able to "dial in" the life signatures while looking at numerous candidate planets in close-by star systems. He found to his amazement and certainly to the amazement of the telescope operator that positive signs of life were on almost all planets that were Earth-sized and in the habitable zones around stable stars.

It sent chills down their spines when the first signs of life were found. The telescope operator could not reveal to anyone about their find until papers were published. Marshall had to sit on the data as well until it was turned into a very carefully worded paper and revealed to the other scientists and then to the public. What many people over the ages had dreamt about had now finally been proven. Science fiction works in the form of books and movies were never seen the same way again.

The reactions to the news had been swift, both negative and positive and would earn Marshall a Nobel Prize in Physics, something he never dreamed of.

For now though he was driving down the road in the middle of the night, not knowing exactly where to go, with the whole world about to catch up to him and change his life forever. It was overwhelming and he realized his heart was racing and his mind ablaze. But for what? All of this energy was understandable but not very productive. All at once he realized that somehow things would work out for him and his angst was unnecessary. He slowed the van down to just below the speed limit and rolled down the window.

The air was fresh and clean, the sounds of driving now comforting, the future not as scary as it was a few hours ago. He made a conscious decision to not look at the clock until the sun came up. He also made a decision to turn back when he felt like it and return to his home.

Hours went by peacefully now, the sun had risen and more people were now on the road headed for their jobs. It was noteworthy to him that people on the road at this time of the morning are not fully awake which shows in their driving skills.

As he came up to a stop light he looked over at a woman waiting for the light to change, they exchanged glances, she had no reaction and when the light changed, she drove quickly away. "I wonder how long this is going to last?" He thought. Will I become a recognizable figure and have to hide most of the time? Will I be hounded?

The publication of the discovery was due out in a few days. He braced himself and appreciated his obscurity, brazenly walking in public places and appreciating being ignored.

The news was then released and as expected there was a significant amount of press coverage. Other experiments were devised to back up his findings and once there was no doubt, he was invited to TV shows, to meet dignitaries and to write a book about his discovery.

What was unpredictable in all of this was that he still remained in relative obscurity after the excitement had died down. Scientists knew of him and much of the population had heard his name. But within a month after the announcement, he could still go into public areas and be left alone. In fact, while driving one day, he saw the same women he had seen at the traffic light when he had come home from his sojourn. She still ignored him. This made him smile as he realized that although he was in the history books, his life would be somewhat normal.

The reason for this, which he did not realize was that most of the people in the world had always expected this discovery to be made. They felt that it was inevitable and therefore unremarkable. Foreign countries carried the news on their channels, it was hot for a week or so, then just old news. This was a far cry from the expectations of people in the 1950', 60's and 70's where aliens were thought of as scary creatures either out to eat you or take over the world and make us slaves.

Well, there were worse things to worry about these days. Water, food and a clean environment were getting scarce. The rich had become richer, the poor poorer and the world smaller via the Internet. News was always in snippets and rarely not

7

editorialized. Facts were no longer as exciting as postulating the possible meaning of them.

So he found himself one day feeling obscure, not in that rarefied place of appreciation and wonderment. Was he disappointed? He wasn't sure, neither place was comfortable although now he had the option of more freedom in his intellectual pursuits. He did not have to perform based on his past work. People weren't looking at him to milk his discovery and capitalize on his fame. He was neutral now. What next?

His options were to continue down the path of discovery and tirelessly work at finding more. Many before him had done that, dedicated themselves to their scholarly interests up until the point were they could no longer read or write. Another option for him was to live life, be satisfied with his work as it stood, be that line or few lines in future textbooks and just smile and move on. This option sounded appealing as he could for instance purchase a sailboat and sail the high seas sipping the power from the wind and waves.

Of all of his options, he chose this one and soon found himself at a local marina researching his nautical options. He talked to boat owners, both casual and live-aboard. He talked to captains, full time merchant mariners and read as much as he could about the art of navigation and seamanship. He learned about knots both tying as well as speed. After a few months he crewed on a schooner that plied the Caribbean Seas. This is were he found freedom and knew his heart was directing him to exploring this world in a sailboat.

He purchased a 49' Morgan, with a water maker, GPS and autopilot. He could now select a destination and have the boat direct itself there. This worked quite well when under power with the internal engine but had to be used carefully when under sail. Preferential headings were based on wind direction and currents. He learned how to make the adjustments and soon found himself over the crystal clear waters around the

Bahamas. He could easily see to the bottom of the water, even when it was a 100' deep.

Wondrous, free and full of fresh air, he made his way around the thousands of islands and down the Antilles chain towards South America. The memory of that frantic evening in the van was a very distant defocused set of images and impressions. Life had certainly moved on.

He lived on with salt spray in his face, a slight sunburn and the wildly varying moods of the Ocean.

A month passed, his mind simplified and needed only be concerned with the weather and proper navigation. He felt great and pressed on to seemingly random destinations. This brought him back from Venezuela towards the U.S. Virgin Island and many stops in between.

One day, which proved to be glorious, he was under sail with the mainsail and all of the jibs full and pulling the boat nicely through the water. At this point, The water splashed over the decks periodically and was easily cleared via the scuppers. The jiboom rocked but held true to course, not by autopilot but by his hand on the wheel. A few spokes here and there was all that was required to keep a good track. He was headed towards Puerto Rico, for no particular reason other than it was close and had good food. One of his favorite ports was Arecibo, on the Northern Side, centered on the Island. Winds were favorable on this day to keep his speed up and land in the early afternoon.

He made port nicely, doused his sails and powered into the end of a T dock, where transients were expected to tie up. After securing the boat and shutting down all of the electricals, he made his way to the dock master's office to check in.

"Hola, como esta? How are you?"

"Fine, señor, welcome to Arecibo, I think there is someone to see you here. Please sign this paper and we will take good care of your boat for as long as you stay. I would recommend Lucita's cantina to get your legs back in order, ah, ha, ha."

"Thanks, that might take a while but I could use a good Corona."

"Corona is their specialty, your friend is in the waiting room in front of this building. Adios, señor."

"Adios, gracias."

He had signed the forms, paid a deposit and made his way, a bit wobbly, down a hallway to the waiting room. A woman was there, someone a bit familiar but it was hard to place her in time and space.

"Hello? Were you looking for me?"

"Yes, Marshall, I have been waiting for you to dock for some time, although it seems you had a quick voyage from your last stop."

"True, I did.....you have me at a disadvantage. How do you know me?"

"Its a long story, but I have time to tell it to you if you have the patience."

"Uh, well, okay. You from the media?"

"No, of course not. I have no interest in having our discussion recorded or in fact known to anyone but you and me."

"Fine by me, would you like to sit down for some coffee or a beer?"

"Lucita's is next door and saving some seats for us."

"You read my mind."

She got up and started for the door, then passing through it, held it open for him.

He thought, "well she is certainly complete, but who is she?"

She smirked a bit as if she heard the thought.

"In due time."

"Excuse me?"

She did not reply but continued to lead the way to the cantina. He tried to keep up gracefully but after so many days at sea, his legs were still convinced that the ground was pitching and rolling.

They looked quite the pair as she led him into the bar, spoke briefly to the hostess and moved to a quiet secluded table by the window overlooking the water. She sat down in a confident manner, said something to the waiter and waited for Marshall to navigate to his seat. He almost needed both hands to steady himself.

Soon two Coronas appeared, both for him. She had tea.

"No drink for you?"

"Can't, my system will be very angry with me and I will end up ripping my clothes off and running around screaming."

"Mormon girl?"

"Not exactly, in fact not even close although their idea of star babies is interesting."

"Okay, that's it, who the hell are you? You have either special knowledge or special talents."

"Both."

"And?"

"I am not from here...."

"Not surprised."

"But if you will let me finish, I am from a place far away and have been following you for quite some time now."

Marshall was a bit stunned, too many questions, too many vague answers. He looked at her for a while and then..

"The girl in the car!"

"Several times."

"Why are you following me?"

"We call this 'first contact' and I wish to get to know you well before we send others."

"Uh, okay, help me out here. Where are you from again?"

11

"You call it 'Bernard's star' and it is quite close by stellar standards."

"Quite. So you are from this star, from one of its planets presumably, except this is a bit hard to believe. Bernard's star does not have the most hospitable environment for life. I know it well."

"Actually, you do not know it well at all. Long ago its violent nature disrupted its own solar system, changing orbits and in some cases releasing some of its planets from the gravitational grip they once enjoyed and sent them at great speeds into space. Several of these planets had moons, which although perturbed, continued to orbit their home planets. My planet, Agora, was quite advanced relative to your Earth. We enjoyed peace and spent most of our efforts in research, discovery and discussions. We became what you might be familiar with, a reflection of your ancient Greece, but without the conflicts and war."

"I'm sorry to interrupt but how do you know about our ancient Greece?"

"Once you established your internet, we just spent our time researching your culture with it. We were able to establish several radio links into your internet, we used high frequency links initially but when you started the high bandwidth satellite connections we were able to use those as well. It is remarkable how quickly you increased your bandwidth and speeds. We soon discovered your ancient culture which in many ways was superior to the one you now are part of."

"Yes, I know. However please continue with your story."

She shifted to a more comfortable position and for the first time Marshall noticed a slight difference in how she held herself, it was as if she had muscles in different places in her body; not completely different just subtly different.

"Okay, as it turns out the planet I am from had a moon with an outpost dedicated to astronomy of all types, and by the way, the 'types' that you are familiar with all reduce to one endeavor when you really understand how the electro-magnetic spectrum works. I was on that moon in a research laboratory that was self sufficient in terms of energy and all other living requirements. We had mastered what you call atomic energy and did not need any source of energy outside of mass itself. Our planet was also self sufficient and most of the population survived but had to live in perpetual darkness as the planet moved into outer space. During this process we passed close by a very large planet, much like your Jupiter. Because of the great gravitational forces, our planet and moon were separated. The planet became a moon of the larger planet and we on its original moon were greatly accelerated out of our orbit and sent in the direction of your solar system. As we sped through space, we knew our only chance of survival was to become a part of another solar system, where we could explore and if life existed there, become part of nature."

"How long have you been here?"

"About 100 years."

"And, where were you hiding?"

"On a planetoid you call Sedna. In reality it's the moon that was ejected from our star system and we were exploring."

"And now you think its safe to contact us?"

"Somewhat. The problem is that you have now developed the tools and techniques to look for life in the Universe. Within a short time it was inevitable that you would have found us and probably be shocked at our level of sophistication and close proximity to you. We believe that it is a danger to us considering you still have a significant amount of very destructive devices. Your culture is still quite war-like but we think it is time to start communicating and hopefully you will eventually understand the futility of conflict."

"Sedna is in the Oort cloud and very distant, I doubt that we could be a threat."

"You have sent several space probes into our space and beyond, we believe you have the means to reach us if you so choose."

"I see your point. My next question is how you got here, to Earth?"

"We can produce any material from our moon and the local debris field in the cloud; it was easy to configure robots to harvest the materials necessary to make a ship for this kind of trip."

"Where is your ship now?"

"It's hidden from your radars and sensors. Someday I hope to take you there and show you, but for now I cannot risk the exposure. In fact you must not speak of our conversations in any way until we are all ready to come forward."

"No one would believe me anyway; even with my recent discoveries, people would consider me someone who has lost the ability to be rational."

"We have the means to make that happen...to you."

Marshall stiffened a bit at this news, thought about it, then realized that it was plausible with a more advanced society like her's.

"I'm sure you can give me advanced intellectual powers. I understand and will respect your restrictions."

"Thank you. For now I just want to introduce myself to you. There will be many questions and it is probably in our best interest to get married and live together."

"Hmm...okay. That's a bit sudden, very sudden in fact. Normally we would get to know each other before such a commitment, just in case we are not compatible and would have a hard time getting along."

"We are compatible Marshall, and I assure you we will get along. I will be your Hypatia."

Marshall had long ago stopped drinking his beer and was a bit stunned to find out his life was now programmed for him. He considered her words and affect, but needed time to process this experience.

"What's next, a wedding?"

"No, but that will happen soon. We need to talk further."

"No kidding."

It was now time to finish the beers in front of him and perhaps order quite a few more.

She sat there placidly while he considered her words, looked at her, and weighed his old future against his new one.

"You will be happy."

"Promise?"

"Yes."

"But will you be happy?"

"Yes. Actually I am very happy to be here now, with you. It has been very long journey, several of us actually died."

"How long?"

"We left our solar system when your Plato was teaching at the Academy in Athens."

"And *several* of you died? How long do you live?"

"We're not sure, the ones who died were the victims of accidents."

"Perfect DNA replication. We have a few species on Earth that have that ability. Doctors here are getting closer to achieving the same for humans."

"We know and you will in fact achieve what you seek, however be aware of the consequences."

"And those are?"

"Instant overpopulation, very high stress levels, rampant disease propagation just to name a few. But the most important thing is that you need to be mentally prepared for living thousands of years. This is the greatest challenge."

"I'm sure you're right. I sure would like to try though, so many things I could accomplish."

"I know and have considered those facts. We might in fact give you that chance."

"Hmmm, okay then. I will be on my best behavior from now on. By the way, what is your name? What do I call you?"

"Persephone."

"Persephone? That sounds familiar to me. From ancient literature, uh, oh yes. The wife of Pluto."

"Yes. I chose that name after studying your history and our proximity to Pluto your ninth planet."

"Nice name. I like it. So you think we will be a good couple, huh?"

"Yes, perfect."

"Okay, good. I will take your word on this. So...what do we do next? I was sailing around the world, do you want to join me?"

"Yes, that is the plan."

"The plan? So what else is in the plan?"

"We have a lot to talk about. Mostly about preparing the human race for the news about our existence. We will start the learning process for society and contribute a piece at every stop on our voyage. That way it will not be too sudden and cause panic."

"Okay, so where are we going next?"

"Where you were originally headed, Marshall?"

"Tahiti?"

"Yes."

"And how did you know that?"

"Its in your history books."

"Okay this is getting a bit weird."

He looked at her with apprehension. Quickly she took his hands in her's and within a second the look and the fears associated with it were melted away. He slowly smiled and relaxed. A casual observer in the bar had been watching them and noticed that when she took his hands a portion of her arms

16

became transparent. The observer rubbed his eyes and ordered another margarita.

After another few minutes, Marshall and Persephone rose and left the bar. They went directly to Marshall's sailboat and untied the lines. Soon they were maneuvering out of the slip and into the bay that he had sailed into just an hour or so ago. The harbor master looked out of his window and saw the boat pulling way and thought it was unusual to pay for several nights stay and then leave. He surmised that the gringo had found a lady friend and was just out to impress her.

They did not pick up any provisions or fuel for the onboard generator. They would not require either one. Persephone could supply all needs during their journey.

For many days, they slipped along through the water, always with a tail wind and comfortable temperature. There were no storms or rough seas to negotiate. During the evenings the stars were crystal clear and beckoning. The air was always fresh.

Marshall felt like he was in a trance. Food was always available, even steak and other non seafood items. He was happy and enjoyed talking to Persephone as she described her journey and the old star system. They were indeed advanced, at least 10,000 years advanced. This seems like a large number but is nothing in the cosmic time scale. Their world and evolution took a different track of course and sentient beings were present on their planet well before Earth had them.

This would be a very common occurrence in the Universe

What they had become was telepathic. They were able to sense the electrical impulses in other minds and present a picture or experience that was comfortable for the other species. This worked very well within close proximity to someone else but dissipated with range. At the far fringes of communication the person would sense something going on but not be influenced by it. At great distance the effect was non existent so if

17

someone happened to be looking through a telescope or large binoculars, Persephone would appear to be radically different from her up-close projection. As a consequence, she would hide below decks whenever they were near another vessel.

As a result of these telepathic talents, Marshall was able to absorb an amazing amount of information about her race; in the process she was able to increase his mental capacity to 20 percent, twice the normal value for humans. Going higher than that was not advisable as the onslaught of information and talent could easily turn the person into a very isolated entity.

The real purpose of this voyage was to prepare a human for the arrival of a new race of beings, one highly advanced. The challenge would be to make humanity comfortable and not suspicious or paranoid. This would be no easy task.

He learned that Bernard's star is 10 Billion years old, much older than our own sun, that it is brighter in the infrared spectrum than the visible and at one time astronomers on Earth were convinced it had planets but later analysis proved that this was a false assumption.

What was now "our" Sedna was actually a Dyson's sphere where the moon (about 1/3 the size of our own moon) was hollow and contained a centralized power source in the very center which radiated heat. The surface of the planetoid is actually an insulating layer and helps control the heat within. The surface is also used to absorb the billions of hits it endured during its flight to our solar system. As the bits of rock and dust pounded the surface, their remains added to the depth and thus it became stronger as it flew though space. Surface radars found the larger objects which Sedna avoided by maneuvering. On Earth radio astronomers misinterpreted these radar transmissions as Pulsars.

Once Sedna was captured by the Sun's gravitational pull, it remained in orbit for many years undetected as it watched us by listening to our radio and TV emanations amongst other things. It would see our nuclear tests and see the bright flashes of our laser weapons. Sedna was discovered by our scientists in 2003 on Mt. Palomar using a telescope completed in 1948. It moved to a highly elliptical orbit which will be circularized in the near future. It is the intent of the Sednans to announce their presence and if all goes well, fly their planetoid to the asteroid belt to continue the building process with the debris there. They also intend to colonize Mars. Sedna is also a very red object as the water and methane on the surface created a significant amount of iron oxide.

They sailed for over a week to get to Tahiti, but it was worth the effort. First they sailed south from Puerto Rico through the island chains and eventually to Panama. The climate changed from tropical to muggy as they entered the canal system to make their way to the Pacific Ocean. Heat and mosquitos covered them. Initially Marshall was very uncomfortable. He was also almost incredulous watching Persephone cooly move about and never complain about the bug bites. At some point he had had enough and asked the obvious.

"Persephone, how is that you look cool all of the time and don't seem to be getting bitten by all of these bugs?"

"Simple, I lowered my body temperature 10 degrees and excrete a noxious repellent from my pores."

"Ok, I find that hard to believe."

"Would you like me to show you how?"

"Absolutely, I'm dying here."

She moved closer and carefully placed her hands on his head. He started to hear a buzzing sound and lost his ability to concentrate. Within a few seconds he actually felt cool and a few seconds after that his skin was damp with a slightly yellow fluid. The bugs would attempt a landing but within a foot or so, flew away erratically. Instantly he felt much more comfortable. She took her hands off and smiled at him.

"There. Better?"

"Wonderful ! Thank you."

The buzzing had stopped and he felt rejuvenated. Basking in his new comfort he walked back to the helm and continued sailing through the rivers that led to the Panama lock system. He smiled at her, as she smiled back.

"Pluto," he said.

"Pluto?"

"Yes, you should call me Pluto."

She knew the reference, paused to look at him for a while and then continued with her work.

Pluto was Persephone's husband in the Underworld. She was a part of both Greek and Roman mythology. Known for fertility and for changing the seasons, she was also known as someone who did not like crowds and preferred to work and live on her own. This is how Pluto (or Hades) found her and took her into the Underworld against her will. He took many things against her will. At best she was able to live above the ground for three seasons then had to return below during the course of a year. Marshall recognized a few traits about the myth of Persephone that seemed to be reflected in her modern counterpart. She certainly did not like crowds and retained a watchful stance at all times, even after they got to know each other pretty well.

Maybe the reference to Pluto was not that funny of a joke. He prudently decided to let that fade into history.

They sailed on and as they found themselves on the downhill part of the journey, Marshall had changed (or had been changed) quite a bit compared to when he had first met her. His demeanor was more serious, his thoughts crisp and focused, his goals clear. As he had spoken and learned so much from her, he had therefore been transformed into a person with a mission. Initially the details were hazy and grey although the energy and dedication were overwhelming. Soon enough, the exact details were revealed and he was properly programmed to execute his directive.

A day or two later they arrived in Papeete, Tahiti. A few miles offshore, they ejected all paperwork, serial numbers and the name of the boat to completely keep the boat from being traced. As there was no float plan, no one was looking for him, or them for that matter.

They tied up at a lonely dock, removed their belongings, spartan as they were, and proceeded into town. They walked separately, one far behind the other, directly to the airport Marshall booked tickets to Tokyo, Persephone to San Francisco. They never spoke during their walk to the airport and would not speak to each other until they met again in Oldavai Gorge, Tanzania, home of some of the oldest remnants of human civilization.

They chose to travel in opposite directions, to set up meetings and educate astronomers, philosophers and statesmen about their new outworld cousins. The plan was to discuss the similarities and differences between the species and to facilitate future collaboration. This had to be done without future shock, as the Sednans were significantly more advanced.

"Any advanced technology will appear as magic," said Arthur C. Clarke. So too were the Sednan's capabilities. To avoid frightening people, it had to be suppressed. They not only had technological advances but more importantly they had species advances They could read people's thoughts, even modify them. In fact it was near impossible for them to leave a room full of people without a permanent sense that something special had just occurred.

They had to be careful. Persephone was more adept and talented but Marshall was just learning about his recently acquired talents.

Around the planet they went in opposite directions, leading meeting after meeting until local press coverage started

21

to take notice. Scholarly articles and papers were written as well discussing the merits of their claims. The scientific community was skeptical of course and took to verifying the new information with space telescopes and large observatories on the ground. Sedna is so far away that this was a difficult process and within several months the community was discussing the improbability of the idea that more advanced beings were so far away. The time had come for a demonstration which Persephone had to perform. She had anticipated this turn of events and had timed her program for when she met Marshall at Olduvai.

Why Olduvai? Because it was known as the cradle of civilization, where a two-million-year old ancestor of homo sapiens had been discovered. In fact, her name was Lucy and was found by Mary Leakey in 1959. The anthropologists were able to determine the developmental and social advancements of this ancient culture by examining the bones and tools of this group of hominids. It was also a very remote site in Tanzania, Africa which would be a private as well as poignant place to coordinate their activities.

They met after having spent many months traveling. The world was abuzz about the claims of the aliens and became a mix of curiosity as well as anxiety. Interestingly, there was a pause in aggression and warlike activity, which social commentators and futurists had anticipated long ago. We were now all one species bracing ourselves for the introduction of another, strange and advanced group of beings to appear. There was tension.

Once they had established a base camp, Marshall and Persephone planned their coup-de-gras. This would entail revealing the ship that brought her to this planet. She chose to do this in London, England, just over the Thames. It flew down from near the North Pole, creating aurora and sonic booms as it flew revealing an electromagnetic propulsion system of significant strength. This in itself caused a great stir. Once over England, the radar scopes lit up with its signature which before entering the controlled airspace was not detectable. The craft made it's way to London and parked itself over the Thames near the parliament buildings, neither getting too close or making any sound. The only sense that it was there was a feeling of a large magnetic forces being applied to keep it hovering in the air. Ferrous materials moved slightly and all compasses pointed in the general direction of the craft. Radio and television transmission frequencies also shifted slightly making communications sound like a squawking duck.

All of this was performed by remote control as Persephone somehow could connect with the craft and direct its movement.

After an hour the craft moved off to the South. Jet fighters had been deployed to photograph or protect their territories. They followed the craft until it was over water, where it accelerated so quickly it was impossible to keep up with. At the point where the pilots lost visual contact with the craft, the radar signature also disappeared and all that remained was a series of sonic booms that seemed to come from all directions.

After the display, the world was convinced of the advancements of the Sednans, but unsure of the next chapter. Marshall and Persephone were gone as far as the rest of the world was concerned. In fact they were watching from Oldavai and when the time was right, Persephone recalled the ship (which at this time was hidden in the deep ocean) to where they were camped, they boarded and Marshall, by some unknown means, knew to walk to a cubical within and enter it. The door shut and he remained motionless from that point on. Persephone went to the cockpit area of the craft, sat down and remained motionless for a moment. Screens showed the rapid progression of news and discussion about the demonstration. At the appropriate time she moved her head slightly and screens appeared showing other life forms unlike her own. Within a few seconds, they started to change appearance to a more humanlike form. Her head moved back to the original position as the craft now started to move vertically, then tangentially to the Earth until it was in orbit and weightless. Unlike other objects that we had hurled into space, it was capable of remaining exactly in position no matter what the altitude. It remained parked over London at an altitude of about 100 miles to observe. Again, there was no radar signature or any other way to detect its presence.

The noise and drama settled down after a week or so, Persephone detected this change and started the next phase of the introduction. Within hours, many ships similar to hers arrived and landed on Earth. They did so in a precise, even geometric pattern. The Sednans within them emerged and quickly took control of the population, sending most people to cubicles similar to the one Marshall was now in.

The amount of communications, internet traffic and energy usage fell quickly to near zero.

The remaining humans were brought to a covered, indoor arena in the United States to begin the process of assimilation. This was not in the sense of domination or producing robotic worker bees. This was more like having their minds opened up for full use. The Sednans were very selective with regards to the remaining humans, choosing those who were capable of allowing the expansion of consciousness and awareness. These included a cross section of human endeavors including artists, engineers, philosophers, scientists as well as a sampling of most other occupations. The brains were allowed to use all of their capability, initially this came as a shock, but soon they realized their new powers and would never want to go back to their old existences. This was reminiscent of the story 'Flowers for Algernon' where a person was operated on resulting in much greater intelligence. A shock initially but he was much happier after the change. So too were the humans who went through the process.

Now the two species were compatible. Once "programmed" the humans interacted flawlessly with their new neighbors. Significant changes happened around the globe, which was inevitable within the normal course of human evolution, it was just accelerated by the Sednans. Borders disappeared, populations were controlled, science and knowledge advanced.

The humans who had been stored in cubicles were released slowly back into the population.

One of the very last to be resuscitated was Marshall. He awoke 10 years after the last meeting with Persephone. She was there when he first sat up, cleared his eyes and recognized her.

"Persephone!"

"Hello Pluto, welcome to the Underworld."

NINA

"Life is not a problem to be solved,
but a reality to be experienced." - *Soren Kierkegaard*

She went by Nina and heard that word most of her life. A gentle friendly soul, who under all circumstances would prefer to give than to receive. As nice as a human could be, it was her defense mechanism, her identity and her wish. Because the majority of humanity did not share her quest, she often became victim to those who were not so giving. One

26

night, during her last year, she succumbed to the wishes of her sort-of boyfriend. She died at 32. He wanted to party and drive fast that cool Florida evening. Nina held on and prayed for it to be over, but he drove faster, yelling and drinking and acting like he wanted out of this world. Down the Northbound highway they sped, around annoyed drivers and within the view of highway bystanders. He was showing off his Nascar skills, except he did not have Nascar training or mentality. Within minutes of hitting 100 miles per hour, some unaware driver changes lanes, not realizing someone behind them was going 60 miles an hour over the speed limit. Nina's car swerved, the back end lost traction and the well worn tires gave up their fight to stay in control. Seconds later, the car was inverted, six feet off of the pavement and heading towards the 40 foot steep embankment that led to the river below. The car was dark inside as seen from a few horrified onlookers. The roaring sound of the speeding car was replaced by near silence, save for the air being disturbed by the metal not designed to fly. It went over the side, tumbling now, and ripped down the brushes and vines attempting to co-exist on the embankment. A spark was created within the crunching metal and the fuel vapors from the spilling gas ignited. By this time, Nina could not tell where the sky or ground was as both images swirled in front of her like the view out of a plane spinning vertically towards the ground. They hit something, which crushed in the passenger side of the car, including the seat belt release mechanism. Fire and smoke were coming into the car as it continued to release its kinetic energy. The car pounded itself into the interface between the embankment and the river, now enveloped totally in fire. They were still conscious, gathering their wits and trying to allow their spinning brains to stop. He released himself and without looking at Nina, crawled out of the car and stumbled away. Nina, watching him, could not release the seat belt, thought her last thought, "I am glad he is safe," and burned to death.

Dreamily, something hovered over the accident site which was still on fire, and watched people rushing to the scene, calling on their cell phones, attending to the driver. The heat from the inferno had long ago melted the paint from the car and lit the area up with bright orange light. The hovering continued, moving perspective around the area without thought. It could not hear, smell or feel anything. It just existed somehow in the gradient of life that is projected on certain parts of the brain after the light is detected and organized by the eyes. It was that conformal film of being that was left, non-corporeal but eternal. It watched the fire, the people, the road, and the sky above.

Soon the carnage was cleaned and mother nature did what she always does, take over. Within a few weeks the accident scene had leaves and flowers upon it again. The family belonging to Nina placed a marker, "Drive Safely" and left several dozen flowers, mostly red and white, her favorite colors. These flowers were hardy and nearly permanent, as they were plastic.

Years later the hovering consciousness had observed the seasons, many thousands of cars, dogs, cats and people on walks along the riverside. It was neither bored nor excited, for those were the emotions of living humans, not the spirits which would remain from those special people in life like Nina. On occasion she could move closer to birds and animals to see their detail. Along the way she had also learned to hear, smell and sometimes feel things, although it was as if these senses were now placed in different parts of the brain. At times it was also possible to move away from her habitat and follow someone for many miles. It was just dependent on whether or not she was interested. On the most rare occasions she could also make conditions right to move something. It was a boring life for the most part, but a life nonetheless.

One day, she hovered about watching a sunset and icly watching the cars go by, when a man on a walk passed by her flowers. He had been there before a few times, but this time he stopped and looking at her name on the cross, spoke it out loud. "Nina Ann Staffort." He paused in thought and moved on to finish his walk. As was her ability, she followed and listened to his mind. He wondered about who she was and what had happened. He also felt that her time must have been too short on Earth, that she was probably young and probably nice. Although he did not know for sure, he felt that this was an accident of mis-spent youth, unaware of why it's so important to savor all of the days you have. Youth sometimes brings blindness and deafness as the sense of omnipotence overwhelms the truth about life's frailties. Such were the events of that night, he guessed.

Nina took interest. She had never experienced a person like this. He seemed sensitive, caring and intelligent. She followed his mind from musing about her and her plight to the design of spacecraft, which took up most of his time. She decided to stay with him and guide him, or probably better said, "give him..his quest". It was her nature to do so and she committed herself to the task.

After he had an evening's rest in a local hotel, where she waited patiently for him to awaken, she followed him to his car, watched him start it and went to work with him. This was the first time she felt comfortable in a car as the last experience had not gone so well. He drove carefully and was completely aware of his surroundings. This allayed her fears about experiencing another accident even though it would not have had any effect on her.

At work, he ran calculations, spreadsheets, simulations and models of spacecraft operations. His job was to design these structures, test them and watch them roar into space to make yet another foothold in the climb to becoming a space faring society. It was the natural order of things and he was proud to be a part of the process. His ambitious nature kept him close to the real action but not in the club of those few who were more qualified and/or lucky to have gotten there first. A component that he designed that would for instance allow humans to go to Mars would be a fine accomplishment, even though he would rather go himself.

She could not help him with the math and science, but she could help him with circumstance. She would give him the "luck" necessary to give him a chance to fulfill his dreams. There are many aerospace workers that work hard but never have a chance to be a part of history. He would experience the path so many deserved yet never get the chance to experience.

He worked late and even on weekends sometimes. He worked hard in an effort to do the best job, but did not focus on advancements. In a way this is admirable but in life there are quite a few ambitious types that will take advantage of good workers and use them for their own good. Its human nature and in aerospace, you can be an astronaut by being a test pilot and then obtaining a PhD, or you can become a project manager or world renown principal investigator and take responsibility for the creation of a spacecraft. In many cases, it is the ambitious that thrive. These are the quickest ways to being a part of the journey to space. Behind each type is a thousand support staff. The only way for one of the chorus to become the lead is to achieve spectacular recognition and have significant luck. Such would be case here.

He worked hard by habit. One day, his supervisor came in.

"Your analysis of the thermal properties was very good. We will use it for the final model dynamics and would like you to present the results to the staff during the critical design review."

"Thank you, I look forward to the presentation."

Within a few weeks he wore a tie and made his presentation over a fifteen minute window when his section came up
during the review. It was a dry review of the distribution of
thermal energy during launch, orbital insertion and final po-
sitioning. The design he had produced assured the safe transit
of the spacecraft, in this case a satellite, from launch to orbit,
without overheating or cooling too much.

Nina was there and with her ability to sense the thoughts
of those in attendance, found one of the high level managers
who was thinking that he was presenting a competent analysis
of a serious issue in spaceflight. She presented an image to
his mind that the presentation was an indication of greater
capability within this engineer. After the design review, about
a week later, this manager had an opportunity to make a decision regarding a position opening for a design manager for a
future manned spacecraft. He chose the thermal engineer.

The thermal engineer, Stephen was his name, was thrilled
and relieved that all of his hard work had produced something
of value. He was called into the "mahogany row" office a week
later. This was where the upper management resided. The big
decisions were made here, decisions that could change the
course of people's lives. He was called into the CEO's office
one Monday morning.

"Please sit down. Coffee?"

"No thanks sir."

"Let's go with Jonathan."

"Okay Jonathan."

"Stephen, your work has been exemplary, as is most of
the engineers' at this company. Something we and the stock-
holders are very appreciative about. But in your case, and I
hope you don't mind if I come directly to the point, there is
something special going on. I can't remember ever having so
many accolades and recommendations coming from the upper
management about one particular person. I needed to meet

31

this person and evaluate how he, you, could best fit in this company."

"I appreciate the good words, Jonathan, how can I help?"

"Well, we have been contacted by NASA recently about a very ambitious project that includes a flight and an exploration of the surface of Titan. This will be one of their first attempts at hibernating a human being for several years. They have done it in the laboratory successfully, but this time they want to try it in space. By the way, Stephen, all of this that I am telling you is classified. Classified at the highest level. Do you understand?"

"Clearly."

"As you probably know, in 2004 a satellite probe, "Huygens" dropped down through the atmosphere of the moon Titan, which by the way is half again as large as our Moon, to find rivers of Methane and volcanic activity."

"Yes, I remember."

"Well, data from that probe and subsequent research from our ground based radar telescopes has revealed the probable existence of life on that moon. This has been deemed privileged information and cannot be distributed to the general public."

"May I ask why sir?"

"Because there are radio signatures that we cannot explain coming from that moon."

"Hmm."

"So the powers that be have decided to put out a classified Request for Quotation or RFQ. We are not by any means the largest aerospace company that is on the distribution list for this RFQ. I am hoping that we will be the smartest. That's where you come in Stephen."

"How so?"

"You are like Richard Feynman moving up in the world with your innovative designs and creative solutions to difficult problems in satellite design. You probably don't realize that you have written the book for the understanding of the thermal properties of man-made structures in space. You also might not realize that your approach to distributing heat has had an added benefit in protecting living things from the radiation in space. Your approach of uniform layers of protection and thermal dissipation lends itself to the use of water, used often in your solutions, to protect the electronic components and it happens to be the best solution to protecting people as well."

"Water has a lot of benefits, I discovered."

"And that is an understatement."

"So can I help with the RFQ?"

"Actually, we would like you to lead the effort."

"I am honored."

"Well, this is no trivial affair. We have reason to believe that we have the right combination of people and technology to win this one and it's worth billions. So there is a lot of interest. Do you understand?"

"I do."

"Well maybe you do. I want you to assemble the very best of our people to work on this. We have thousands of engineers and scientists, some who are well respected in their fields. We will provide you with a staff to evaluate all of our talent and assemble a powerful team of experts. Its extremely important that we win this. Do you understand?"

"I certainly sense the urgency. Can I ask why?"

"All I can tell you for now is that it comes from the top and what I mean from the top is that the top tier aerospace CEOs met with the President at a undisclosed location to discuss the matter. I was one of the participants, lets leave it at that."

"Understood."

"Good, your office is now just down the hall from mine. Your staff is being assembled and will have the kick off meeting in the 'War Room' in two days. You will chair the meeting.

Everyone attending will have level nine clearances. I will be present via video link. Get your people together and ride them hard."

"Shall do sir."

"Good, dismissed."

Stephen rose and feeling a military atmosphere, turned formally towards the door and exited. As he emerged from the office, many eyes from the surrounding staff were upon him. They knew something significant was going on, and that he was the key.

He walked back to his old office and found it cleaned out. Workers were filling in the holes, preparing the dry wall and masking the surfaces for paint in anticipation of a new tenant. He asked where his books and files were and was told:

"Don't know sir, we're just following orders."

Stephen walked down the hall and found an acquaintance. They had no idea what was going on except for the fact that Stephen was moving.

The only thing to do was to walk back to Mahogany Row and try to find his new office. He was intercepted halfway by an administrator who if anything exuded conviction.

"Please follow me, Sir."

"Okay," he said looking at her and wondering what was going on.

"You are now in Building One, I am your assistant Kathy."

"Nice to meet you, Kathy. This is all happening very quickly for me. Where is my office?"

"It will be on the top floor, corner office with a nice window."

"That sounds nice."

"Oh it is. Also, you have a staff meeting tomorrow morning at eight."

"Okay, sounds like things are going to be moving quickly."

"No doubt, there are a bunch of engineers and scientists flying in tonight for the meeting. Several have been asked to relocate. You have priority one now at the company."

"Wow, okay, well keep me straight okay?"

"You have nothing to worry about, just do your magic and the mission will be a success."

Stephen thought about these words and their consequences. "All I have to do is my magic," he thought. Not a trivial task. They walked back to Building One and up the stairs to his floor, then to his office. It was five levels above his original pay grade and initially he felt way out of place. Kathy introduced him to his immediate staff, who were placed in areas surrounding his large, corner office. They were polite and focussed. Finally, he was able to sit down in his new chair, Kathy departed to take care of details and the room and his life became quiet. Taking some deep breaths, he examined his oak desk and rotating left, looked out the window at the campus of a multi billion dollar aerospace company. As he did so, the felt a cold change in the area around him. He felt something he could not articulate but it was definitely there. Taking in another deep breath, he decided that it was not threatening, just a presence. He allowed it to envelop him without fear and not knowing why, he made it part of his being.

Later, he was able to start work using his new computer and start the process of organizing the proposal. Something told him to work hard and not worry during the formation of the quotation. The art of delegation was going to be the greatest challenge as so many very competent people would be on the project in the next few days. The first order of business was to go through the resumes and start assigning tasks. This process lasted several hours, after which Stephen decided to start the basic outline of the project. By the time he finished thinking and writing this out it was well after closing time. He rose and headed for the door. A slight dizziness was present as he started to move but it quickly dissipated. Leaving his office, he turned left and headed towards the stairs. As he walked down the hallway, he found several other people in their offices working on various projects. That was the interesting thing about getting those large salaries, sometimes you had to earn them. He descended the steps and walked outside to a cool, dark night. In the distance, he saw his car and began his walk towards it. On the way his mind was at peace and easily dealt with the sense that someone was watching over him. So be it, he thought, better to have someone or something on your side than not. The subject left him as he looked at the stars and once at the car he reached for the door handle. Nina, he thought out of the blue. There was no context or meaning of the word, it just came. He stopped for a moment and for no rational reason, decided to adopt the name as his mascot. Nina.

The next morning he was ready for the meeting, this time in better clothes and with a tie and coat in his new office just in case. At eight the staff meeting started. He found his way to the head of the table (cherry by the way, with nice chairs), sat down and watched the others file in, some acknowledging old acquaintances and some looking right at Stephen to ascertain what was about to happen. As in compartmentalized security situations, very few would know the whole story, only bits and pieces, just enough to define their tasks. Stephen would have to discuss these tasks with the people individually. For now only the overview was appropriate.

"Welcome all, my name is Stephen Daedelus, formerly of building 19, thermal analysis section. I have been given the task of managing the writing of a proposal to address the requirements of a government organization, NASA in this case, in conjunction with another government agency, whose name will be kept out of this conversation for now. What should be understood is that our direction in this matter comes from the very top. You have been assembled here to write chapters of this proposal germane to your expertise. You will have all the resources you require to complete your tasks. The good news is that we have a very strong case to win this, the bad news is that we are not going to lift our heads and relax until it is complete. This includes several peer reviews and a preliminary design review. I will need daily reports from your group leaders and weekly high level meetings with everyone. The fuse is short on this one. I have created a shared space on the central computer system to give everyone an idea of the context of this proposal. Go to your sections and begin the process. Keep all of your work in the file space given to you. This includes all research items, e-mails and notes. Nothing will be stored in your personal computers. Read the project overview presentation first. Any and all questions should be e-mailed to me and my immediate staff. You will find this project fascinating and challenging. Few of you have ever worked on such a large and important project. Keep working hard until you are finished, no distractions. Finally, nothing I have discussed leaves this room. Okay? Lets get started."

With that command they all rose and moved towards the doors and to their offices. Stephen stood up to see them out and tried to make eye contact with all of them. Most he could see were deep in thought about the road ahead and what they would be required to produce. After they had all left he went back to his desk, signed into his computer and found the office number of the first engineer he would have to brief. Turning to his left he looked out of the window and thought about starting this process and what results it would produce. Rising, he walked to the door and out of his office. Outside the sun was warm, a few clouds hung in the air and he reminisced about flying through them in a small plane a while back. It was a rare sense of freedom, flying amongst the clouds carefree. These days would be different as the project would consume enough time to keep him out of the air...at least for now.

He met the first engineer, a communications specialist. They found a secure room and sat down to discuss the particulars of the engineer's assignment. This would be chapter three and appendix five. Once the engineer was brought up to speed, he was allowed to ask any questions regarding his task after which they parted company and Stephen proceeded to the next engineer. The rest of the day was filled with visits much like this one. The whole story in Stephen's head and the constituent parts in theirs.

Within a week, the shared space on the main computer cloud was filling up with details. Once each engineer was done, a copy of the completed work was added to the draft proposal.

Within a month, the draft was complete and the first peer review was held. Changes were made, the language was smoothed over and the completed second draft was given to a panel of independent reviewers for comment. This next step produced red lines which were discussed and added to the document. Finally, the proposal was complete and ready for submission. A lot of overtime had been spent, certainly by Stephen and the immediate staff, to complete and polish this document. Copies were printed and the CEO was advised that they were ready to move forward.

Jonathan called Stephen into his office soon thereafter to thank him for his work and advise him of the next steps.

"I am taking the corporate jet to Washington tonight with this proposal, I will call you tomorrow if there are any questions. Thank you for your hard work."

"Of course, let hope we win this one."

The CEO looked up at him smiling and said, "I have a feeling....."

Stephen did not know exactly how to interpret this comment but came away from the meeting with a sense of confidence based on the CEO's reactions. He left the office and walked back to his own. Entering, he stopped half way and staring briefly at his desk, decided that he had worked a ton of overtime in the last month and he could now take a break. He grabbed his keys and left, telling his assistant he was going to be gone for the rest of the day. The assistant understood and simply said, "Relax, you deserve it."

On the way to his car, Stephen felt that presence again, comforting and warm. He sat in his car for a second, looking at his office window, started the car, rolled down the windows and backed out of his spot to leave. No plans had been made so he gravitated towards his favorite spots which included a marina, the beach and an airport. He made his final spontaneous stop at the airport and walking into the office, rented a plane to catch some air.

He broke ground and left his cares looking up at him as he flew away. There is always that sense of release when one flies, looking down at the people in traffic jams and congestion; there is clean air and freedom above. For some reason there is also the unshackled feeling, where you need to concentrate on something real, not interpreted.

Over an hour transpired as the plane climbed, descended and turned. On several occasions it flew through a cloud. Clouds smell different in the air, which at those altitudes is very clean. One senses the abrupt change in humidity and unconsciously the nostrils of the pilot tend to flare for the best effect. The pilot's eyes move from the outside to the instruments in his plane to keep true. Looking out of the wind screen just before the plane enters the cloud gives the sense of great speed and an impending bump of turbulence but for small clouds turbulence is seldom felt. Pilots also feel compelled to change attitude within the cloud so that the emerging scene looks different from the entering scene. Its all quite amazing when done properly. By the time the pilot has played with the clouds, Earth does not exist anymore. It only is a darkened expanse at some angle relative to reality. Airplanes create their own gravity and thus the sensation of up can be from any angle, even upside down relative to the Earth. In space it is the same effect with the exception of the lack of gravity. After flight all pilots remember the last moments of being airborne just before the Earth locks us down again.

Stephen was there for as long as he needed, then sensing it was time to come back, he turned for home base and descended to pattern altitude. He entered 45 degrees relative to the runway, looking out for other planes and slowed the aircraft down. The noise of air rushing over the airframe started to dissipate. Across from the numbers, he went through his check list and applied the first setting of flaps, slowing the aircraft and initiating final descent. At the 45 degree angle relative to the numbers painted on the end of the runway, the plane turned left, still descending. Again just before lining up with the runway, it turned left again, the last flap setting was applied and the slowest safe speed was achieved. Like a bird flaring just before a landing, the plane's engine was brought to idle and as it slowed it simply sat down on the runway, tail low. The roll out was un-eventful and it exited to one of the taxi ways at a brisk walking pace. Another checklist was completed and Stephen maneuvered the aircraft to a tie down place. It was all over too soon as the sound of the engine was replace by silence. Cleaning up the cabin Stephen opened the door and exited, feeling like he had just returned from vacation, his mind active with the images of gliding with the birds.

After the plane was tied down, he walked into the FBO and paid for the rental. Now he was back to reality as he walked to the car he caught a glimpse now and then of the machines of freedom. The drive home was forgettable as was the evening. The next day would come soon enough as he fell asleep with the faint images of clouds below him as the transition was made.

The morning lacked the memories of this hiatus and he prepared for work, just like a thousand other days. Back to the car and back to his parking space.

One thing that had eluded him over the last 24 hours was that funny feeling of companionship. He shrugged it off not having ever understood it completely. Once in his office however, it did return, in somewhat of a matured state.

The phone rang.

"This is Stephen."

"Stephen, Jonathan. Its a go, time to get serious as we have been turned on to execute the mission."

"We have a mission?"

"Most definitely. Get the troops together and let them know that they are now officially behind schedule."

"Shall do, thanks."

"No, thank you. I am not sure what happened but when I arrived to the breakfast meeting, the decision had already been made. It was amazing, no discussion, no questions, just 'move.'"

"Wow, okay I will get a meeting together this morning and let them know their new tasks."

"Good, see you in a few days."

Stephen put the phone down and looked briefly at where it sat in the cradle. It seemed amazing what had come over the wires just a few seconds ago. He walked out of his office to talk to his administrative team.

"Please get the senior staff together as soon as possible, we have ourselves a mission."

"Good news, Stephen. Congratulations."

"Thank you, but we have a lot of work ahead of us."

41

Hours later, he walked into a medium sized conference room, like many others he had been in, if anything a little nicer. The only real difference was the guards at the door. The other participants were there and looking at him for answers and direction.

"Please sit down," he started, "Guards, lock the room down until I call you."

The guards left, closing the doors behind them and the sound of an engaging lock was heard.

"Okay, here it is....we won the proposal, in its entirety. That means we have to hire about 300 engineers and support personnel. For the next several weeks all of us are going to be interviewing. We need to start with the people holding security clearances as they will be building the craft. Next the disciplines represented in this room need to grow into departments and keep a tight schedule during the process. I have spoken to each of you about your particular responsibility, now you and only you will get a complete briefing. The reason we are in this room today is to build a spacecraft to go to Titan, one of Saturn's moon. This spacecraft will contain several people who we will eventually choose, who have a mission to discover the source of radio static that the Huygens probe and ground based instruments have discovered. The probe, I can now tell you, was active for significantly longer than the public is aware. The government pulled the plug once probe started showing images of motion in several of the onboard cameras. We will now watch a classified video clip from this probe. Please, the lights."

The lights dimmed and the people in the room watched, transfixed as the projected images of a multitude of ant-like creatures came into view, sometimes moving randomly as Earthly ants do, and some lining up in very particular shapes unlike anything the engineers and scientists in the room had ever seen. For a while it seemed that no one was breathing.

"They're intelligent."

"Yes, we believe so."

"How intelligent?"

"Enough to transmit modulated radio waves as a particular frequency."

Silence followed this admission.

"I thought the atmosphere was raining methane and the surface temperature was below -300 F?"

"It is, in fact, the possibility of life in that environment is amazing, unless of course there are pockets of warmer atmosphere near the surface, our temperature measurements were not that accurate during that mission. Our concern is more about the radio emissions which are AM modulated at 1 MHz and have a sophisticated repeating pattern. We need to find out what it is."

"Have we tried to respond to the transmission?"

"Getting through Earth's ionosphere at 1 MHz is very difficult and yes we have tried but we can barely detect their transmissions here with even the best radio telescopes. Therefore it should be at least as difficult for them to hear us. Another important detail is that we have thousands of AM radio stations around that frequency, which pollute the data. In actuality our probe's mother ship, Cassini, was equipped with low frequency receivers to be used for other experiments. We were just lucky enough that the receivers could record the emissions at a reasonably high rate and for a long period of time."

"What's the plan?"

"Design, build, test and launch as soon as practical. Get your people together, we will start having the high level meetings tomorrow to discuss the entire scope of the mission.

With that decree, they adjourned and prepared for a lot of work.

During the next several weeks, they consolidated the design into a working model that the software simulators could put through various tests to make sure the approach was viable. Essentially they were designing a very thermally stable spaceship that would support the life of three astronauts who would be placed in hibernation over a period of several years. After this period they would wake to start the process of examining the moon in detail over the course of several months. Then they would reverse the process and return to Earth. The whole mission could take up to seven years, even with the fastest propulsion available. Stephen's knowledge of thermal design was the center piece of the effort as they had to preserve every millidegree of heat to keep the spacecraft habitable. In addition, they had to protect the crew from radiation which is very intense in inter planetary space. His approach was to keep things simple and take advantage of resources available on Earth. The main one of interest was water. The fundamental design was to encapsulate the astronauts in a spacecraft surrounded by a thick layer of water. This had been used successfully before in various space stations and nuclear power plants. As it would quickly turn to ice in space, it would also provide a protective coating for small meteorite impacts. The thickness of this layer would be several meters, filling in gaps and covering the conformal surfaces of the ship. The concept worked well both in theory and in practice once they started the real assembly of the ship in orbit.

Soon the ship was mostly assembled and Stephen started spending more time in space than on the ground. It soon became home for him. Interestingly, he still could feel the presence of a guardian angel, much like he had so many times before. This brought him comfort even though he knew these feelings were more irrational than scientific. He also had the new sense that he had been very lucky over the last many months, coinciding with the feeling that someone was looking after him.

Soon the ship was complete and Stephen was fully prepared to start the journey, most of which would be spent in hibernation, as it would take years for the craft to make its way to the Saturnian system. The other astronauts were fully prepared as well and eager to get started. Even with ion propulsion the craft, named Huygens II, would take well over seven years to make the trip. The astronauts would take turns being "awake" to monitor systems and communicate with mission control. Most of the time two of the three would live for about a month before retiring to their deep sleep chambers. The experiences of the International Space Station came in handy here. Proper training and astronaut selection created a well balanced stable team that guaranteed the best chances of success.

After a brief ceremony and many goodbyes, the astronauts entered the ship one by one; Stephen was the last. As he transitioned from the ferry capsule to the vast insides of Huygens II he felt a cold breeze followed by quiet. It made him stop for a moment to consider what it meant. But he knew what it meant, his companion and good luck provider was leaving him. This made him a bit anxious as he would need luck on this trip.

The spirit, Nina, had more work to do however. She had helped Stephen and gave him the breaks few obtain. He was living his dream. It was now time to return to that highway and cluster of plastic flowers to await another opportunity. Such was the purity of her essence.

The mission went well, they discovered the source of the radio waves from the Saturnian moon, which left them with more questions than answers. Stephen in particular was transformed when they arrived, as he felt the presence of the same curious sensations he experienced back on Earth. It was generally described as an energy of unknown source and strength. Although they did not know the total strength of this power, they did discover that it was growing at the same rate as humans expired on Earth.

WHAT FUTURE HATH WE WROUGHT?

"In the twenty-first century, the robot will take the place which slave labor occupied in ancient civilization." - *Nikola Tesla*

There are few great jobs in this world. Most people enjoy theirs and get up in the morning to spend years at their particular occupation. Some stay for decades, some for days. In general it seems that one needs to resonate with an occupation, not deal with the wasted time of politics and proceed into the future with hope. Hope was once defined as looking forward to a comfortable retirement, but greed took away that option. The greed of the capitalists, inherent in their construction and merciless in their pursuits. To ask them to share would be like asking a starving dog to stop eating. The hard earned money placed in retirement funds and other investments followed the familiar path of gambling, with the same returns. Everyone wanted to hit that 21 but few people did. This left the majority disappointed and the very few happy. The happy ones were following their passions and did not think of their daily activities as labor, although they were getting paid nonetheless. Russell Fox was one of the lucky ones and rolled out of bed each morning to get to work early and explore the Universe.

Russ's job was to be an explorer. He worked at the reincarnation of NASA, after it had failed as a converter of money to science. It had been caught trying to make everyone happy, the scientists, the bureaucrats, the politicians and the taxpayers. Once the public had asked why the federal budget set aside 4 percent of its income to develop all of the hardware and software to go into space and land on the moon. This had included the development of satellites and advanced aerodynamic components to fly us to our destinations. It had included advanced communications and enabled the first transcontinental and transoceanic communications. The public saw the Olympics staged in Europe from the reflected signal off of a giant balloon (Echo I and II) designed by NASA. They performed how we wanted our science to perform, by moving us forward as a people. Then the budget was whittled down to .04 percent of the federal budget and was plagued by cost overruns and slipping schedules. At this point the ax was dropped, the scientists were the vast minority of the job force, having been replaced by management, accountants and lawyers. What remained was a cadre of specialists, leaders in their fields and a budget designed on R&D and spread across many governmental departments. NASA itself was a shadow of itself but still operational on a few successful, acceptable, and inexpensive projects. Russ worked for one of these projects.

His occupation was to operate a telepresence machine for eight hours a day, explore Mars and the moons of Saturn as well as operate the 100 meter optical telescope placed on the moon.

The cost of having humans go into space was too great to be handled by the managers. They did not have the driving force of a Werner Von Braun to keep them in line and working hard. Von Braun kept everyone's attention during his most influential period. One of his failings however was to trade federal money for senators' wishes; he broke the fundamental NASA departments into regional centers spread across the United States. This gave good jobs to many people but slowed the progress of discovery way down as shipping, time zones and mis-communications took their toll. NASA had recognized this fact only too late and brought the space agency back to Cape Canaveral where it belonged. Here Russ went to work, entering a building and farther inside, to blackened stages where technicians communicated with satellites or robots sprinkled about the solar system.

The solution to further research had been in the recognition that telepresence was the only realistic option for space travel. It was far cheaper and certainly safer. For now it dominated the discovery race. Also, it was the best option for the next chapter of space exploration which was the designing and building of a very large space ship that would spend years traveling the cosmos. The hardware and software needed for such an audacious project were being developed in the offices and laboratories still standing from the Apollo era on the Cape.

Russ would walk down these halls, following the footsteps of the great scientists and brave astronauts of the past. Their pictures still adorned the walls to remind the workers of their purpose. The hallways were of a typical government building style with concrete blocks and white paint. Many had crypto doors where only those who had been briefed were allowed to pass. Russ walked past these and into another highly secure area, where human guards greeted the entrants and checked their credentials. They always gave Russ a serious look when he entered and always checked his badge electronically as well as visually. He would pass through and then into one of several crypto doors to his final destination. This would be a large room with black painted walls, kept to the lowest practical light level. The only better lit area was in the center where a 60 foot sphere was placed covered with wires and fiber optic cables. This was Russ's office and where he spent the majority of his time. He almost always smiled when he saw this sphere, as he knew that someday he would no doubt witness something new and probably fantastic.

Checking in with the technicians and engineers, he made his way around the monitors to check the health of the machine and its present connections. There were numerous probes and robots around the solar system which sent the visual, aural and motion-sensing information back to this sphere at very high bandwidths. Outside of the time delay, there was near real-time feedback and control where the operator could allow the robot to move autonomously and input desired changes that would be integrated into the robot's natural movements. It worked pretty well, especially when the robots placed on the surface of some world could sense certain minerals or fluids like water. In that case they would do what the operator would have done in any event and make measurements or gather samples. The artificial intelligence software was quite sophisticated by now, anticipating moves and decisions by their operators. As a result many times the operators were simply observing.

The robots had performed most efficiently in building and gathering raw materials. When asked to do so they built multiple dwellings on the moon, completed an astronaut camp on Mars, mined and shipped incredible amounts of minerals from the Saturnian mcons. The success of these telepresence robots revitalized the public interest in space exploration. NASA took the hint and placed smaller robots on the lunar and Martian surfaces to allow college and high school students the opportunity to explore as well. These efforts were largely successful. Finally, the general public was allowed to participate via the Internet (for a small fee of course).

Russ however, had the best job, as some of the robots he controlled were massive and covered with sensors. On Mars for instance, Russ controlled a robot with 12 arms and 64 eyes which stood 10 meters high. Within minutes it could dig a 30 meter hole and harvest the ice within it. The ice was then melted and sometimes turned into fuel to be used to power the beast. During the earliest stages of the mission, they had programmed the robot to build bricks by placing soil in a mold, melting ice into it and allowing the ice to re-freeze within it. The bricks were formed into a wall, then a room, then a building. The bricks were sealed into place by again melting ice over the surfaces using lasers. Depending on the number of applications, the surface could be many centimeters thick and extremely strong. All of this was done without human control. Once Russ started to pilot the robot however, the decision was made to complete the building and upon the reception of several construction packages sent from Earth, to power it, light it and form an atmosphere within it. A greenhouse was also built that allowed the growing of lichen, moss, algae and small plants. Within months of this activity, oxygen began forming to a human sustaining level. Further chemical conversions from oxygen refineries sent from Earth built, stored and regulated the air into a perfect environment for real humans to visit. It was when this task was complete that Russ gct a new assignment.

"We want you to be the general contractor," declared his supervisor.

"I'm not sure I understand," commented Russ.

"The new excitement from the general public is allowing us to make the next bold step into space. We would like you to supervise the construction of a very large space ship in orbit."

"Fantastic! I had always hoped this day would come. When do I start?"

"Kick off meeting is in two days, preliminary design review in two weeks, critical design review in two months and then you will get very, very busy."

"Whoa, short fuse on this project, huh?"

"We need to move quickly to show progress to the public and based on the advances you and your team have shown us, we feel confident that you can get the job done. It will be a 24/7 activity. The good news is that we are developing an extremely sophisticated robot for you to control. The bad news is that we are going to make seven hundred of them. These robots will initially be human made and programmed, then they will start making and programming themselves. They will be sent out to a rendezvous area just a few miles from the International Space Station, or what is left of it."

"Do you think that is wise? I mean, to have robots make so many copies of themselves and allow them to do their own programming?"

"We have a multitude of internal controls to make sure nothing gets out of hand."

"Yeah, I've heard that before."

"Yee of little faith, we have come a long away from those virus prone Unibots."

"Well, okay, but I need to be careful nonetheless, this appears to be a very important program."

"Indeed it is. The operational manuals are in your cloud-space folders. Train the students to operate the outlander robots and get started."

"Aye, Aye."

Russ looked up at the sphere and considered the future. Building an entire large spacecraft, that would be a challenge. Training a robot to train robots could be a nightmare.

He gathered the students and gave them the good news. They scurried off to study and train to take over Russ's duties. Russ went to his office and started to read manuals. Manuals that would change his life.

Many hours later, Russ was ready to get started and walked to the sphere. He instructed the technicians to connect to the robot factory where the first advanced robot was being designed. The engineers there had already created a simulator for the purpose of fine tuning the telepresence and feedback. Russ thought it would be a good idea to get in the game early to allow him to watch the progress and potentially make changes as they got underway. Once the techs were done with their connections, they gave him a nod and he entered the sphere. He worked his way to the center via removable walkways and took his place at the control panel. The walkways retracted leaving him in a complete visual environment where every view from the robot could be seen. His first impressions were good and he contacted the communications technician.

"Clency, the image quality is exceptional."

"Yes, sir. They use over a hundred 23 Megapixel cameras that stitch the images together. We can zoom in quite a bit and with some added software extrapolate what a high resolution image will look like at higher zoom limits. The effect is like moving through space instead of just magnifying the image. We also have sound, smell and tactile feedback."

"Nice. Sound and smell probably won't be of much help in space but the tactile feedback will be necessary."

"The sound and smell can be configured to be sensitive to electrical activity like radio transmissions or infrared etc."

"Very nice. Okay lets give this simulator a little workout."

Russ grabbed the hand manipulator and could see an arm reaching out towards a table with several devices on it. One of which was an electronic box with connectors. The communications technician called on the intercom:

"Russ, we have installed a new system. Put on the gloves in front of you and just move your hand and arms around, the robot arm will follow."

"Wow, okay."

Russ put the gloves on and noticed that as he put on the second the image of the robotic arm was following his move. Once the other glove was on, two robotic arms were moving in complete synchrony with Russ's movements. Russ could also sense small pressures in his palms and fingers. He move carefully to pick up the electronic box on the table and could, with high fidelity, feel the box, its weight and its balance.

"Man, that feels great. They really have figured out the tactile sense algorithms."

"That's true, and it still is improving as the software engineers improve the details of this system. You will be able to do brain surgery with this someday."

"Someday soon, no doubt."

Russ moved around and watched the robot arms repeat his every move. The image was retinal, or so high in quality that you could not tell that it was not real. Soon, he felt a part of the scene and subtly sensed that there was sound involved with the faint perception that he could hear the motors in the robot as they articulated the limbs. He put the box down and realizing that he could walk about the synthesized room and proceeded to do so. He moved within the sphere and the robot moved in a room. He found a door, opened it and walked through. He walked down a hallway looking around at people in their offices and walking down the hall and by the robot. It was completely convincing and he realized then that making a spacecraft with this kind of telepresence would be easy. All he needed was building materials and tools. Turning around he found his way back in the original room and took the gloves off to stop the simulation.

"Absolutely amazing", he said mostly to himself.

"Best I have ever seen," came the voice of the technician.

A bit startled, Russ came out of the sphere and walked over to the control panels where the technicians sat. He paused a bit then said,"

"Can you image what we can do now?"

"Anything, anywhere."

"The only thing I did not try was the autonomous routines."

"We can arrange for that tomorrow if you would like."

"Sure, that works for me. It will also give me a chance to read some more of the manuals."

It was like flying a new plane, where you studied before you went into a simulator. Then the idea was to used the scenario-based learning approach to handle normal and abnormal routines. In this way the pilot (or operator in this case) could be trained to handle all contingencies. Russ picked up more manuals than he could read and absorb then left work to study at home, where he would not be disturbed.

The next day he entered the sim again and started to become comfortable with the system. He spent hours in the sim sphere and explored as many aspects of the robot's capabilities as possible. After that and the next several days he spent getting competent and then expert in operating the system. It became second nature for Russ to operate the robots and became as easy as normal life to interact with the amazing visual representation and tactile feedbacks. At some point Russ actually became lost in the experience and felt like the robot was actually him. This was due to a special set of subroutines that was learning as much from Russ's interactions as Russ was learning from the sim. Curiously, Russ felt particularly drained after these out of body experiences but also strangely drawn to them. On a few occasions, the technicians had to come in and get him as he had become so absorbed he forgot to come out for lunch or go home in the evening.

Russ passed the Preliminary and Critical Design Reviews with ease. They then went into high gear.

Once the robots were deemed qualified, NASA started to launch supply ships into orbit carrying the bits and pieces for a significant structure. Eventually, hundreds of rocket launches would be required and the original international space station would be dismantled for building materials. This was all part of the re-use program implemented at the space agency, scooping up defunct satellites and orbiting debris that had so polluted near Earth space. Most of the materials were made of exotic materials and had been tested for long life and dependability.

NASA also sent up the first phalanx of robots to start the process of organizing and assembling the initial structures.

At this time Russ was the lead controller and performed the initial operations to get the robots on task. As with the simulator experience, he noticed that they seemed to get more and more competent as time went on. Initially, they would follow all commands and wait until asked to do something further. Later, they would go beyond their initial commands and finish jobs they had performed before. If left alone, they started to enable themselves and perform tasks that were slated to be done in the future. Eventually, Russ noticed that he could simply command them to build a complex appendage to the spacecraft structure and they would complete the task unaided. To an extent Russ was concerned as he did not know how far the learning behavior would go. The software engineers were delighted of course to see their hard work come to fruition. The crown jewel of their efforts was the autonomous subroutine Russ had recently become aware of. This routine was a combination of a software optimizer and a free will algorithm. It was the brainchild of one of the lead programers, Eric, who had carefully organized the script for robotic behavior that reflected the eventual desires of the controllers. This was done predictively initially, when a 'look forward' routine designed the optimal pathway to success. In this case success was defined as the completion of the spaceship.

Eventually, Russ and the other controllers became more monitors than manipulators. Everyone, especially the managers, where happy about the progress, as the building of this complex structure was taking less time and therefore less money to complete. In fact, it appeared that if they let the autonomous routines have full authority, they could reduce the entire project effort by a third. Once this detail was realized, the upper management made a decision to allow this to happen.

Russ by this time was getting more concerned as something in the back of his mind told him that the robots could in fact build the structure more efficiently but because they would then transition to members of the flight crew after the craft was complete, he wondered how well they would transition to taking orders again. Eric had produced a learning machine that would continually enhance itself based on experience. Whatever the goal was became the uncompromising focus of the machine. With perfect memory and GigaHertz thinking rates, these robots might soon consider humans to be a detriment.

There had been a precedent for this type of behavior. In the United States, the engineers and designers had made amazing creations, then in an effort to lower the cost and maximize profits, these products were made by other countries. This built up and eventual demise brought down many cultures. Price was the driver, not necessarily the human condition. The idea

57

to take the least expensive path or put another way, the idea to define the human goal based on financial worth, moved the human direction away from self improvement and the quest for knowledge and understanding. These quests simply cost too much as the people would be worth more as they became designers and creators and less interested in being workers. The need for workers was always higher. Robots now were the natural extension of the cost first philosophy. They not only took over the role of worker but were now taking over the role of creator. Russ was one of the first to realize this fact. He envisioned humans becoming second class citizens. The robots would be able to do everything better, including evolve.

As he continued to work and observe the robot workers, his concerns came to fruition. On a cold bright day in January, Russ went into the simulators and discovered that overnight, they had all changed assignments and position.

"What happened?"

"We are not sure, they are not responding correctly to commands."

"What do you mean 'responding correctly'?"

"I mean, they are receiving our commands and acknowledging, but they have set a different priority and will not cease operations."

"That's not good. They won't even accept a re-boot command?"

"No, sir. However, their work rate has increased 15% and instead of one robot working on a single task, that same robot is working on several tasks, depending on what is in his particular area. They limit movement that way and all robots now have all skills."

"Does there seem to be a central command center?"

"No, sir. They have all distributed the central command structure and each processes a particular thread in parallel.

As a result their combined computing power is several magnitudes greater."

"Wow, but you say they still respond – but do no act on our commands?"

"Yes, sir.

"Okay, we need to get Eric to create a virus to stop this operation. Does anyone know where he is?"

"Yes, he is having meetings with management. I'm guessing he had the same idea."

"Okay, good. Hopefully we can get something done quickly. I don't like how fast this is progressing."

For the next several hours, they watched the monitors and documented any new changes to the robots' programming. The individual robots were working at their maximum power capabilities, moving as fast as they possibly could within overlapping spheres of work areas. At one moment, a robot was assembling a structural member of the ship, the next the same robot was wiring the area in anticipation of the neighboring robot finishing the wiring or structure in it's area. It was amazing to witness and impressive to know that they had increased productivity so much.

Eric returned finally and bringing everyone together sat them down.

"I have just returned from a meeting of the top managers in the company that built the robots and NASA. I described the situation and made them clearly aware of the dangers of letting this go unchecked. They considered the options, weighed the impacts on the shareholders, workers and general public. They have decided to allow the robots to act autonomously. I objected vehemently but they told me that I did not understand the whole picture. As a result, we are to observe, document and not interfere. They are assuming that when the job is complete the robots will stand down and return to normal."

Russ interjected, "that might not happen, Eric."

"No I do not think it will, not with their present strength and computing capability. In reality they have far surpassed the human brain and more importantly, will continue to improve. In another few weeks, right about when they are predicted to finish the ship, they will all be super-robots as compared to what they are now. I cannot predict what they will do."

"Can you make a virus, just in case we need to get control of them?"

"Yes, but it probably won't work."

"Why do you say that?"

"Because we discovered that they have been scouring the Internet at Gigabyte speeds and have already formed defenses for every virus out there."

"How ironic. We need the very thing we have been fighting for so long. And now it is not powerful enough to help us."

"Yes, we have been ordered to not interfere or we will be terminated. The company thinks the advancements we are witnessing will have a future in new products."

"Eric, this is a nightmare in progress. I suggest you work on the virus in the meantime. We will monitor and report to you as needed. Hopefully, I am wrong about this but 'it ain't natural' if you know what I mean."

"Oh, its natural Russ. Just not natural in our way of thinking. We could be witnessing the birth of a new species. One that could potentially advance us ten fold. It could be a very good thing for us."

"Maybe, or it could be a disaster."

"We will know in a couple of weeks."

With that decree, they all went back to work, some excited and some concerned.

Within a week and a half they got their answer. Predictably ahead of schedule. The robots had completed the space station using every scrap of space debris and the entire International Space Station. The ship looked mostly like the original design by not exactly. Several critical components had been modified, including the environmental controls, which were set to operate the internal areas of the ship at much cooler temperatures. One by one the robots were moving inside the ship to evenly distributed spacings. Then they attached themselves to a bulkhead or wall and shut down, with the exception of a very low level communications sub-routine which apparently would let them wake up again if commanded. At the point there were only a handful of robots left, the massive internet stream was shut down. The ship then powered up and started to move out of orbit.

An emergency management meeting was convened where Russ and Eric relayed their findings and proposed ideas to gain control of the ship. Eric had in fact created a virus but by the time he had permission to try to upload it, the robots on the ship had shut down the communications system. There would be no point in interacting with humans anymore as it simply was a power drain.

The ship gained speed and all the scientists and engineers could do was watch it with their telescopes as it disappeared into the cosmos.

TELE-PRESENCE ON ANOTHER WORLD....

"I visualized a time when we will be to robots what dogs are to humans. And I am rooting for the machines." - *Claude Shannon*

The probe hit the atmosphere at 25,000 miles an hour and instantly heated up to thousands of degrees. The g forces rose above 10 and as it streaked through the skies, it was witnessed by millions. They had expected it and with a mixture of curiosity and trepidation watched it do exactly what it said it was going to do.

A thousand days ago, radio astronomers received modulated signals from a particular part of the sky from a satellite purported to be from another world. It sent out signals that included video, data and sound which repeated every 10 hours. The transmissions included a primer to decode the data and piece together the pictures. After translation, the inhabitants of this world found out that this probe was from another inhabited world known as Earth, many light years away. It was to land in the ocean and continue to beacon until it was found. The purpose of the probe was to establish communications with the inhabitants of this planet, known to the Earth people as 'Bernard's world' because it was near the very close star called 'Bernard's star.'

The probe did as it had advertised and landed in the ocean just a few miles from the coast of an inhabited continent. Soon ships were dispatched to retrieve the probe. These ships had some of the scientists aboard who had learned the language of humans, in this case Esperanto. They were to keep the probe out at sea until it was determined to be safe. The military equivalent of this world was also alerted just in case the probe's intentions were malevolent.

The images, sounds and data that was broadcast in the days before its arrival included not only the language primer but pictures, movies and music from Earth. It was intended to come in peace with the hope of establishing long distance communications with the radio astronomers on Earth. Instructions were therefore included that described the assembly of many antennas that in concert could establish the link. The designers of the probe realized that other beings would not necessarily have the detailed knowledge of electromagnetic theory and the technology to make integrated circuits, transistors or vacuum tubes for that matter. The transmitter and receiver for this apparatus had to be simple at least initially for there was no way to evaluate how sophisticated the inhabitants would be, but with a crude setup, at least an acknowledgement of the probe's successful landing would be helpful.

The apparatus was a modified spark gap transmitter and a receiver made of silicon and germanium. It was assumed that wire would be available.

All of this was a plan "B" arrangement just in case the probe telemetry system should fail, at least there would be a crude way to communicate.

After the probe was retrieved it was brought to a large building much like a high bay laboratory on Earth. It was placed in the center and monitoring equipment set up to follow its movement, if any.

The inhabitants were actually reasonably sophisticated and had electrical systems, high quality farming, communications and astronomers.

The probe was programmed to scan the spectrum for radio waves, listen to any stations it found, listen to its surrounding, take pictures and by the use of artificial intelligence, make a decision as to when to deploy.

After about 24 hours, the mechanism in the probe was activated and as the people in the lab watched and backed up, it slowly opened like a rose and deployed cameras, view screens and touch-pads. The view screens showed the video that it had been broadcasting during the latter stages of its journey. After the video, the view screens encouraged the watchers to push a particular button on the touch pad, to acknowledge that they were present. One of the scientists who had spent several months learning the language from the primer stepped up and pushed the button. The view screen showed someone smiling and then slowly described what the intentions of the probe and the people who designed it was.

The lights dimmed and a holographic projection device placed an image on the floor just to the side of the probe. The probe was also designed to have a telepresence system that showed a scientist back on Earth who would be able to interact directly with the people on the new world. This could be done in real time based on advances recently made in quantum computing, where data could be transferred instantaneously over great distances. The probe then asked if it had permission to proceed.

The scientist discussed the idea with his colleagues and typed the proper commands to begin the projections.

The lights were dimmed and an arm from the probe moved from its top portion horizontally to a place about five meters from the side. Another arm moved from the bottom portion of the probe horizontally and stopped just opposite the higher arm. A hatch opened in the side of the probe and light from each arm and the side illuminated a large space between the arms. The resolution was very good and lifelike as images of fruits, animals and landscapes were projected in sequence for calibration purposes. The laboratory lights were dimmed as much as practical to see and hear the images. The controls were intuitive for the scientist and he could easily interact with the probe.

At the end of the calibration sequence the probe spoke to the scientist.

"Can you hear me?"

"Yes!"

"What is your name?"

"Dar."

"My name is Percival."

"Welcome to our world. We are anxious to know more about you."

"Thank you. We are happy to meet you and have made a great effort to get to your world. We discovered it with our radio telescopes (images of the telescopes were being projected at this time). You are close to us in a relative sense but it still took many years to reach your world. We come in peace and want to establish a dialogue with your people to discover who you are. Several of our scientists will be projecting an image (it was showing an example now) of themselves and they can interact with you to answer questions and transfer knowledge. Do you find this acceptable?"

After a few minutes discussing again with his colleagues, "Yes, yes of course."

At a laboratory back on Earth, the scientists and engineers were adjusting their monitors and fine tuning the signals from the quantum computers. They had built a spherical projection system where the operators could stand inside and see, seamlessly, the images around the probe on Bernard's Planet. They could see the reaction from the people there and view the scene from many different angles. Within time, the probe could deploy drones to fly around the lab on the planet or even go outside to explore their countryside. Initially though, it was decided to take small steps and not get the people there anxious. They selected a particular scientist to be the face of Earth, she would stay in the projection sphere with the projection cameras on her for eight hours a day. She had a script to work from that would allow her to teach the inhabitants how to make technologies that would allow them to advance, such as medicines, computers and the like. However she had to first establish where they were intellectually and what natural resources they had to work with. This would take time and would depend on their willingness to work together.

The scientist, Kathy, came in and sat down at the table in the projection area and began to review her notes. A technician indicated to her that the process was about to start and that due to the nature of quantum communications, there could be delays between the two worlds and to be patient.

"Okay," she said. "No problem, I have been briefed about the process."

The technicians continued to adjust the light levels and sound balance as she sat. Once they were satisfied, they indicated that they were now on the air.

She looked up in the general direction of the images projected from the other side.

"Greetings, my name is Kathy. I will be working with you over the next few months answering your questions and getting to know you. We have a lot to talk about." She smiled into the cameras.

"Greetings I am Dar, a scientist on our world we call Sohu. Thank you for sending the language primer, in some ways your language will allow us to better describe ourselves to you."

"We would like to understand your language as well. You may send the details through the data channel we have sent to you. We ask for other details as well; these would include information on your history, technology, family structure and government. We will provide the same."

"Of course, thank you. We now understand your data structure and will start sending the information soon."

"We understand if you need to be careful about transferring sensitive data, we will do the same, certainly until we get to know you."

"Yes, but we are a trusting species and assume you mean no harm."

"We mean no harm and come in peace."

Kathy noticed that the data stream had begun from the planet Sohu. It would be handled very carefully and kept separate from the Internet in case it contained (even inadvertent) viruses or software bugs. She signaled the technicians to begin our data as well.

Sohu was a world much like our own with several interesting differences, the first most obvious was that their version of dinosaurs had thrived and had somehow coexisted with their version of the primate. They became interdependent and worked together towards common goals. Their dinosaurs varied in size greatly with the smaller versions walking on two feet primarily. Like our ancestors their version of the primate evolved into a highly intelligent biped and learned long ago how to farm and domesticate other animal species. Their language evolved faster and became more articulate so that the dinosaurs who learned from the apes and were capable of hunting and more physical labor.

Historically there had been disputes between the two species but now they had settled into a peaceful coexistence, embracing their differences as just other talents. Now with the advent of the probe from Earth, they were interested in yet another species and took the lessons from their past to set the tone of the communication with the new people. There was no reason to start off with a sense of distrust.

Earth on the other hand was a bit more cautious, especially in the light of how biology from different species usually was incompatible. This idea was not from the point of mating but from the huge amount of viruses and bacteriological agents humans and Earth animals bring along with them. This bio-cloud protected us but made us dangerous to others. There had been many examples of isolated groups being nearly wiped out due to common ailments from the visitors, like influenza, small pox, etc.

For this reason the Earth scientists were very interested in the DNA structure of the people on Sohu. Luckily they were advanced enough to produce a complete genome and send the details to the Earth scientists. At the same time a detailed genome from humans was sent back to Sohu. This was actually one of the first scientific priorities for both cultures.

Meanwhile the hologram was getting lots of attention on Sohu from scientists, engineers, politicians and normal people alike. Kathy could see the steady stream of people that moved around her projection, she smiled at them and periodically asked questions. They had similar personalities as those on Earth, caring for their young, working jobs, having hobbies and just generally being curious. Kathy was periodically replaced with others, sometimes in groups to allow many people to see a cross section of our species. Although most of the Sohuans did not understand the language, many tried a word or two to show their interest. Sometimes the participants on the Earth side spoke the language of Sohu to show respect.

After several weeks of transferring information and getting to know each other, the Earth scientists asked to have a private meeting with the medical people on Sohu. They were granted permission to do so and gathered at the appropriate time to discuss a problem they had found.

"Greetings, I am Dr. Chernowski. This (he was pointing now) is Drs. Smith and Bopaul. We are specialists in genetics at a large medical facility on Earth."

"Glad to meet you, Drs. We have a few principal medical people in this room now as well; how may we assist you?"

"We have been examining the genome you sent us and have some concerns."

"Yes, we have been looking at the details as well, we might have a problem."

"We believe so, although it was our intent to get to know you by establishing contact and setting up communications; we also had intended on planning a visit. Several of our people had started training for a long space voyage and were going to fly to your planet within an Earth year. We are very concerned that it would be dangerous for both our people to do that."

"We agree, it is a sad truth that to meet in person could cause extensive biological destruction on our planet and certainly the deaths of your astronauts."

"Yes, our immune systems have each made us safe in our own environments but would be helpless on another planets'."

"Our only hope is to keep our friendship alive by telepresence only."

"We agree."

With that knowledge, each planet sent sterilized probes to the other. They projected images at first then the communications links were infused into robots that were made in each other's image. Within several years, each planet had hundreds of alien representatives walking about in the cities, farms and dwellings of the other. They interacted well with each other and created lasting friendships and professional associations.

It was a great matchup of cultures, interests and common goals; they just would never be able to meet and shake hands.

THE MAYAN POLES

"What a lesson here for our world. One blast, thousands of years of civilization wiped out." - *Mayan quotation*

She set her gear out in a series of lines, like a book with just letters. A mask, flippers, tank, buoyancy compensator, compass, sausage, knife, regulators and wet suit. Everything was checked in detail, as it should always be. This was at the hotel room in Riviera Beach, and she would repeat the same ritual on the boat on the way out to a 50 foot deep ledge famous for great diving. The boat would take a group of divers out just a few miles offshore and drop them off on the southern tip of a submerged reef. The Gulf current would then move them

71

along at a few miles per hour underwater to the pickup point several miles to the North. It was an effortless dive requiring very little energy to glide along the fish-infused waters past great turtles, starfish and a few lazy sharks just to keep you awake. The visibility was usually better than 30 feet as the crystal clear waters of the Little Bahama Bank spilled into this area.

She put her equipment bag on the deck and introduced herself to the other five divers, split between men and women. The captain of the boat, named 'Little Deeper' was affable and very experienced. His boat was very well outfitted with filtered pumps to fill the tanks, food and a decent restroom.

As she came aboard and introduced herself to the others, a small TV on the bridge was showing local activity including weather. The crew kept the TV on while tied up to get the latest forecasts and catch up on game shows, which the captain did not appreciate. Now however, it was replaying a clip just released from NOAA, showing the sun blasting off a huge flare, the greatest one ever recorded. The arc of material that formed was larger than the sun itself, it grew from the equator of the sun and after expanding by at least one diameter broke apart and hurled a billion tons of energetic matter into space. Not just any space but that which lives between the planets. The crew ignored the broadcast warning and tended to the details of bringing the divers on board, having them sign waivers and stowing their gear.

Meanwhile the TV showed noisy images of scientists discussing the details of the solar outburst using charts and graphs, this too was ignored by the crew of the dive boat. What the scientists were showing was their concern for the magnitude of this event. The satellites used to measure energetic particles in the space around Earth were already showing saturation and the true amount of highly charged protons, electrons and radio flux could only be estimated. Some of the sensors went beyond saturation and actually failed; sensors on the Earth's surface which only receive a small fraction of the radiation in space were going into saturation now. Radio, TV and satellite operations were being effected. The next problem would be the power grid which was just starting to go offline in Northern Canada. Although the main cloud of particles was still hours away, the effects could already be seen. For the night time portions of the Earth, amazing auroras could be seen for over a third of the globe. Places that had never seen this phenomena were now aglow with the serpentine strands of light slowly waving it's way through the skies.

The marine radio started to break squelch and produce noise, the captain reached over and turned it way down, thinking that it was going bad. His concentration was now on releasing the lines, casting off and getting his boat out to sea. He applied reverse power to the inside engine on the port side where the dock was and started to pull away from the marina. When at a safe distance he put the port engine in forward along with the starboard engine and cranked the wheel full starboard to make his way to the harbor entrance. He was careful to keep the speed down to not create a wake and disturb the other boats and wildlife that had accumulated in the marina.

Once beyond the harbor entrance he brought the diesel engines up to 1500 rpm to settle into a good cruising speed. The bow came up and they started to splash their way to the drop-off point.

The divers had settled into their respective seats and started the process of rechecking their gear. It had to keep them alive while underwater and so they were meticulous. In addition, once they reached their destination, they would suit up and check each other's gear as a final safety step. For now however it was relaxed and the more experienced told the less what to expect. The trip out would take another 20 minutes. Meanwhile the TV and marine radio had ceased to function properly and were turned off. This meant that the automatic position information coming from the radio was no longer being transmitted. The captain turned on the autopilot to set a course to the primary fix. This was determined by GPS but after a few minutes he noticed that the boat was not tracking properly so he switched to compass heading lock, which was a bit better but still not straight and true as it had been so many times before. He surmised that the problem was with the autopilot and mentally noted to have it tested. While the boat made its way to the primary fix the captain came out from the bimini to look at the sky; this was weather watching activity, a standard for good captains. Although the weather in port was perfect and the forecast good for days to come, he noticed clouds on the horizon, some billowing, which was not expected.

He went down stairs to address the divers.

"Hey everyone, let me have your attention for a minute. We are about 15 minutes out to the drop off point so you can start suiting up now. Also, I notice that the weather might be changing, which was not in the forecast. We will be watching this closely and if we have to go we will come back to where your diver's marker buoy is and circle. This means you need to come up so we can get you safely back to port before the weather hits and it gets rough out here."

He went back up the bridge and noticing that the compass lock on the autopilot was still not working properly. He switched off the box and steered manually. This meant that he would be following the indications of the wet compass, built into the bridge and well calibrated. It seemed to wander more than usual as well, which concerned him. There were a lot of malfunctions going on and this put him in the mode of not taking any chances.

"Hmmm, don't like this...."

Within a few minutes, they reached their destination, a permanent marker buoy was waiting for them, complete with a diver's flag. They slowed the boat and eventually came to a stop ten yards or so away from the buoy. The anchor was released and fell to the bottom about 60 feet down. The winds pulled the boat away from the anchor while the captain let out the rode until it was about 200 feet long, then he secured the line. The anchor dug in nicely and the boat became secure as it faced into the wind. The captain then moved his attention to the divers, watched a bit while they did their safety checks and adjusted their masks, then moved over to the lead diver and spoke to him discreetly.

"Do me a favor will ya? Keep 'em close, instead of moving over to the pickup point, I am going to move off about a hundred yards and keep up with you. The weather is changing quickly and some of my instruments are acting funny. I'll come over if I need to but for now will just tag along and watch things from up here."

"Okay Captain, I'll keep them close."

The Captain then moved down to the middle of the divers, now ready to go in.

"Have a great time, follow your lead diver's instructions and stay safe."

The divers acknowledged his words and made their way to the swim platform at the stern of the boat. One by one they grasped their face masks to keep them from coming off and fell backwards or giant stepped into the blue ocean. The waves were one to two feet, the breeze was light and the sun bright to give good illumination of the reef below. After the splashes had subsided, the Captain made his way to the bridge to monitor the weather and sea conditions. He would wait until the diver's flag, which the lead diver was pulling along with him, moved off at least one hundred yards, then he would weigh anchor and slowly follow along. He would do this with one engine only and keep the rpm as low as possible to keep the noise down for the divers. Sound propagates very easily underwater, so even at a hundred yards, they might still be able to hear the engine noise. Additionally the Gulf current was moving both the divers and boat at roughly the same speed, so it was possible to cut the engine off completely and just drift, but he would not know about this until he went out and took his station.

The time came when the dive flag was sufficiently distant to weigh anchor and move to a safe distance.

The wind was still light, however he noticed quite a bit of cloud build-up on the horizon, a bad sign. The Captain started to listen to the weather channel on his radio for information but again it was very noisy. He could just make out the sound of a voice in the cacophony of static crashes and constant hissing. As the voice was monotone and created by software, he could not tell if there was any urgency in the broadcast. The TV was basically useless as well. He then listened on the common traffic advisory frequency and heard more static. He glanced at the radar and saw a circular front of storms coming at him at a high rate of speed. This was all too much and his mental alarm bells started to go off in his head. The engines were started and he pulled the boat around to retrieve the divers.

Although the diver's flag was not too far away now-about 50 yards-the sea suddenly swelled up about ten feet, then went down over twenty. The wind went from five knots to 50 in a matter of seconds and the captain now had his hands full. The boat heaved, yawed and rolled uncontrollably. It grew very dark suddenly and lightning began to hit the water ferociously. Even with thirty years of ocean-going experience, the Captain was afraid for his life. Most of the unsecured gear had washed overboard and he could not let go of anything to try and get a life jacket, which he knew was his highest priority now. Trying to move along a railing now, the waves were pounding the boat with tons of water and within less than a minute the boat would capsize. He made it around to the cabin, grabbed a waterproof handheld radio donned a life jacket and attempted to return to the bridge. He did not make it to the cabin door before an immense wave hit the boat on the port side and started to spin it longitudinally as it rolled over. He was now underwater and even with the molasses effect of water on movement, it spun like it was weightless. The Captain was lucky to keep his wits enough to find an air tank and regulator even while he was completely disorientated. He thought for a moment that the boat had hit the bottom of the ocean but was unsure where "up" was.

After what seemed like an hour, the motion subsided and all he could tell was that the boat was more stable, although still underwater, and moving along in a strong current. He waited and reminded himself that panic could kill him quicker than anything else now. He checked his air supply gauge and could tell that even with his heavy breathing, the event he just experienced had taken only a few minutes. This made him calm down a bit further and look in the cabin for a stowed face mask. It took a while as the boat was still slowly rotating underwater but he managed to find the mask, put it on and for the first time see around in the water. The cabin was trashed and had a significant amount of floating debris in it moving it seemingly in random directions. He calmed his breathing again and sensed that the motion of the boat was slowing down and that soon it would probably settle on the bottom. For the first time, he thought about the other divers and what had happened to them. Instinctively he looked out of one of the port holes to see if any of them were near the boat. This, he realized, was in vain but he needed to search for them just the same. In all of his diving boat years, he had never lost anyone and even though it was probably impossible given the recent events, he was driven to try and find them just the same.

The boat continued slowing down and did in fact, hit the bottom, about 50 feet down. It slid sideways until it impacted (albeit slowly) the side of a 10 foot reef. Now things were stable and his head, although still spinning, could tell which way was vertical by following the trail of the bubbles coming out of his regulator. He started to assess the situation.

Meanwhile the other divers had heard a very low rumble increasing in amplitude. The diver leader had in fact kept everyone close and after hearing the boat engines start and surge, decided to move everyone to a protected portion of the same reef. There was a depression in it surrounded by coral, he motioned everyone inside and took the safety line and tied it between large rocks and outcroppings to form a small circle of safely line that everyone could hold on to. The sounds became very loud above them and they held on tight as the very large wave action tossed them about even 60 feet below the surface. They held onto the line and each other bracing themselves on the reef to ride out the wave motion. They looked up at one point to see the boat rolling past them as if caught in a breaking wave but underwater. It was a sight never seen by any of them before. The surge of water was immense followed by a very strong current that swept away fish, sea weed and other debris above them. The hole in the reef saved them all from destruction.

After the waves and currents subsided, the diver leader carefully came out of the hole to survey the surroundings. He then returned to the group and checked the air supply of each of them. He wrote the numbers down on an underwater writing tablet. Then he looked up and could tell that the waves were still quite large on the surface so sending everyone to the top would be dangerous. They would have to wait for a while. Their air would start to run out in about an hour as they all had two tanks on that were basically full. He brought them together and using the writing table, told them to stay calm and that they would drift with the now calm current in the direction they saw the boat rolling by. He also checked his compass and discovered something unusual. He looked up and having had quite a few dives in this general area, knew that the hole they were in and another prominent feature on the ocean bed lined up North and South. For some reason, as he looked at his compass, they were now lined up East and West. He filed this fact in his mind for later consideration and went back to his primary task, keeping everyone safe.

He gathered everyone together and as a unit, they ascended to just above the hole to survey the surroundings. The current was back to its gentle self. They continued the ascent until they were clear of the hole and entered the current to be slowly drawn in the direction the boat should be. On the way they saw debris, probably from the boat that included diving gear, charts, electronics and lines. They were certainly on the right trail. As they moved downstream, the dive leader picked up any tanks he found and gave them to the others to keep in case they needed more air.

Within about twenty minutes they came along a reef with more debris near it and finally to the boat itself. As they got closer they could see a bubble trail coming out of the cabin that indicated that someone was in it, hopefully the Captain.

They swam over and started to move around the boat. It was significantly damaged with holes, torn out fittings, broken antennas and broken windows. But within it they saw the Captain looking out of one of the portholes and waving. The dive leader maneuvered around the boat until he found the cabin door. He opened it and moved in to see the Captain floating inside. They exchanged nods and the dive leader took out is writing pad and wrote:

"Glad to see you're alive."

The Captain acknowledged the sentiment and gave the okay sign.

They then started writing back and forth on the tablet to make plans to escape and eventually find their way back to land.

There was an inflatable life raft still bolted onto the boat, several life vests, flares, food in coolers and water in plastic bottles. The plan was to wait as long as possible to let the waves above subside, then tie everything together including the divers, and slowly ascend to the surface. They would use oars, a crude sail and kicking to get themselves back to land. The problem they faced was to find out which way that was. The captain and the diver leader discussed their errant compasses and decided the only real way to safely row to shore was to follow the stars.

More of the divers made their way into the cabin, most carrying spare tanks. They found a small space to occupy and waited there calmly to extend their air supply. The Captain found several more tanks and placed them in the center of the group for whoever needed them.

Over an hour went by and the because the conservation efforts taken by the divers worked well, they still had about twenty minutes of air left each. By this time the captain and dive leader had started to bring together the items they would need on the surface. Using a lot of line, they lashed everything together and gave lines to the divers with use to secure themselves.

Once they were ready they looked around at each other and all acknowledged they were ready to go. They moved out single file from the cabin, waited for the Captain and dive leader to attach the gear to the human train and began the slow ascent to the surface.

The waves had subsided considerably by now but they had no idea what had happened and if it would happen again.

Once at the surface they looked around at a iridescent sky. There was a light breeze that did not smell right and one to two foot waves. They released the CO2 canister's valve and inflated the raft. Luckily it contained survival and signaling gear. They clamored in being careful to not lose anything attached to them and not puncture the raft. Those already inside helped the others come aboard and stow their gear. The raft was certainly big enough for all of them and had been sized to accommodate a full boat of divers. The Captain had been upset that the Coast Guard had made him purchase such an expensive raft but now he was smiling at their insistence.

Once fully inside they took stock of their gear and made sure everyone was okay. Food rations were broken out as well as the water. They ate and drank a bit and put the rest away in case of a long trek back home.

"I can't believe we made it!"

"We're not home yet, we have quite a row ahead of us."

"Which way?"

"We will wait until nightfall to look at the stars and need to go West for about 15 miles. We will row at night"

"Can't we start now?"

"No, the compasses are not working properly, we risk going in the wrong direction."

"What has happened, did you know about the storm?"

"Not at all, it came suddenly along with lost communications and a terrific sea surge, nothing I have ever experienced before. I suggest we all relax and get some rest, tonight we will be real busy."

They assembled a cover over the life raft, found places to lie down in and relaxed-most fell asleep after the trauma of the storm and sinking of their boat. The Captain stayed awake and watched the seas for other boats.

Hours passed and a once-busy area of the Ocean seemed abandoned. It was too quiet, no birds or airplanes for that matter. The Captain thought it strange that the Coast Guard was not even out looking for boaters in distress. He listened to his radio periodically but it was still swamped with noise and basically useless. Transmitting a mayday brought no response. The normally active weather channels were silent. Whatever had happened was significant, possibly devastating.

That evening the ones who were asleep woke up and had their ration of water and food. They had enough supplies for at least a week at sea but hopefully that would not be necessary.

As it got even darker, they realized that the sky was awash with an Aurora. Scintillating waves of color swam above them from horizon to horizon. It was a dazzling sight, one that had never been seen in Florida. They were amazed until one of the divers, a scientist, spoke up.

"This is probably due to that intense solar storm that started a few days ago. Aurora like this has never been seen this far South."

"Yes, its amazing," replied the Captain. "Does this have anything to do with the noise on the radios and the compass problems?"

"Certainly the radio noise can be caused by events like this, however it should not affect the compass, that has to do with the position of the North and South magnetic poles."

"Don't they shift?"

"Yes, but over tens of thousands of years."

Another diver, who was reasonably well -read added, "The Mayans predicted that would happen this year."

The scientist replied, "How could they know about pole reversal back then. They had no instruments to measure precession."

"I have no idea, but its interesting that we are having compass problems when they thought we would."

The Captain looked at the scientist,"Do you think these things are related?"

"Shouldn't be, but again this is all new to me."

Through the waves of illuminescent colors they could just make out the bright stars. They looked for a long while until they were sure they had found the big dipper, then the North Star. Then the Captain said pointing:

"Okay, West is over there, lets get started and I will check out the compass."

They distributed the paddles and started rowing in the prescribed direction. With most of them paddling it seemed like they were making decent progress. The effort however would take hours. Even one mile an hour looks swift when you are right next to the water.

They learned to paddle for 15 minutes then change to another oarsman. The Captain watched the time and the compass which was more or less pointing East. He also kept the North Star off to Starboard hoping that the world was not spinning backwards as well. That would put them in great peril as they would find their way to the middle of the Atlantic Ocean.

Hours passed and most of the rowers were getting tired. The Captain changed the rotation and had half of the people row and half sleep if possible. The rowers would go as long as they could then wake up the other to take over.

Day broke and they continued to make progress. Around 10 am someone said "Look!"

"Is that land?"

"Maybe! Keep rowing! Just pace yourselves, don't over do it."

They went on for another hour and amazingly what they thought was land was indeed land. They instinctively started rowing faster once this was confirmed.

"Pace yourselves. That land could still be miles away."

They did as he asked although not without a dirty lock or two. The last mile was agonizing but they were intent on making it. All that could row did.

Finally as their strength was about to give out and their muscles were burning, they realized that they were in shallow water. A few jumped over board tentatively and after touching the ground in the first time in a day and a half, smiled. Others jumped in to cool off and they all felt a great sense of relief. They pulled the raft towards the beach and finally with a last great effort, up onto the sand and away from the water by about 50 feet.

"Wow, made it!"

"Yes!"

They high fived each other and started looking for some shade to sit under. As the majority of the divers made their way landward, the Captain and scientist walked slowly after them and looked up and down the beach.

"I don't see anyone," said the scientist.

"No, this beach is abandoned."

"That's impossible unless we messed up and somehow landed in the Bahamas."

"Don't think so. I know where that reef is relative to the Florida coast and we are definitely near the coast. There are no buildings, just debris and broken branches."

"Yes, looks like mounds of debris on the horizon there," he said while pointing.

"Hmmm, this is not good at all. I suggest we rest up a bit and walk inland in about 30 minutes, all of us together."

"Agreed."

They joined the others and discussed their plans. One of the divers had brought the radio with her and after listening for a moment said:

"Still just static on all channels."

"There are no people, no planes in the sky, its eerily quiet. What's going on?"

"Not sure, but there could have been a major radiation event. Radiation comes in several varieties, most short lived," the scientist reported. "Its possible that we were protected while we were under water. NASA has known for years that water absorbs radiation very effectively and they have designed spaceships that have safe areas which are surrounded by water, for the crew in the case of high radiation events. We need to go inland and find out what's happening and exactly where we are. We will need food and water soon. We also need to make sure that its not contaminated, so don't eat anything yet. I will try to find a way to tell if its radioactive.

"What about fish? They are underwater."

"Maybe, as long as they are not eating debris that has washed down from the land. We need to be very careful."

"How can we tell if things are radioactive then?"

"We need a geiger counter, a smoke detector or a cell phone. The geiger counter would be the best."

"How will a cell phone detect radiation? We probably can find one of those."

"Radioactive particles cause the pixels on the phone's camera to turn on. If we put the phone in a completely dark area and take a picture, the number of speckles will tell us if there is radiation."

They decided to wait until the heat of the day had passed, then they would venture together inland and see what had happened. For now they just waited and sweated.

As dusk arrived they readied themselves for a hike. Wetsuits were cut to make shorts and short sleeve shirts due to the temperature in Florida making it necessary. They had to cut their flippers to make crude footwear. They brought whatever they felt was really necessary and after looking at each other, started the trek into "town," whatever that would turn out to be.

After leaving the beach they found the remnants of a highway with large amounts of debris and the hulks of building and houses. There had been a catastrophic event here. It looked like a huge hurricane had passed over and had scraped the land almost clean.

They walked for another hour into what used to be a downtown portion of a city. Again, debris was everywhere but curiously they found no human or animal remains as they walked. In the distance they could see the remnants of what looked like a control tower at an airport. Deciding to explore that area, they walked towards it and after another hour, came into the airport grounds. Again the area had the look of having been scraped clear; the remnants of the control tower still stood strongly as it was made of two-foot-thick concrete. The top still had most of the cab intact with only a few blown out windows. They decided to climb the stairs and use the cab as a lookout point, both to see what was left of the city and to see if anyone was still alive out there.

The climb upstairs was long and arduous as the tower was over three hundred feet tall. The insides of the tower were dark and there was more than a little apprehension about finding bodies up there. The scientist in the group assured them that by rule, the tower has to be abandoned when the forecast or current conditions go beyond certain limits. He also mentioned that most if not all towers like this airport one had backup power systems in case the main power went down, and it was certainly down. During their hike the silence was deafening. People get used to the 60 Hz hum pervading everything; lights motors even wiring. When it is gone, for instance during a power outage, there is a obvious sense of quiet. Gone too were the sound of cars, trucks, airplanes and trains. It was truly quiet, even the sounds of wildlife were missing.

They finally made it to the cab and guessed that the controllers had left in a hurry, for there were still some uneaten hamburgers which, even though almost two days old, where quickly devoured.

"Do they have refrigerators in these things," one asked?

"Yes, and rest areas and I am looking for the emergency power system...ah here it is."

He pushed the start button, then a green "active" light illuminated. Next he flipped a large switch to transfer the power from grid to generator. Lights came alive along with radios, the radar and a beacon light. He turned off the light and most of the radios to save power, then checked the environmental systems. There was a fresh water tank, air conditioning, heating and an intercom.

Rooms below the cab were explored, several refrigerators were found with MREs and other food. There were more radar screens in these rooms as well.

"This is the local TRACON, approach and departure controller stations, this must have been a pretty active airport."

"I think you're right, quite a few people worked here."

Others explored the rest of the tower but this time using one of the elevators to move between floors. The locked the bottom access doors as a precaution.

"The emergency fuel looks full but we will need to ration it. I suggest we keep a radio on the emergency contact frequency as much as possible and periodically use the radar to see if anything is flying out there. It has a range of well over 100 miles. The radar will act like a radio beacon to any others out there as well and periodically we can call out on the emergency channel. Also we have the rotating beacon light on the top of this tower, we can turn that on periodically to get anyone's attention out there."

"This airport probably has a lot of fuel somewhere, we should look for the tanks and keep our emergency power tanks full, just in case."

"I agree."

"And we will be safe here, this tower is very strong, certainly made it through whatever happened here."

"Absolutely, we should also post a lookout in the cab to watch out for whatever might still be out there."

"Good."

"Alright, lets clean this place up and make it our home for now."

They split up and went to the several floors available to tidy things and make sleeping areas. Most chose the top floors with windows to sleep in and help look out. The very top floor had a broken window which they replaced with some thick plywood that they had found for that very purpose. The size was cut correctly and there were latches to hold it in place.

There was food enough for at least a week, then more would be needed. But for now, they had a central place to call home that would protect them from the elements at least until they discovered what had happened.

The silence outside was deafening even as night rolled in.

They decided to keep the cab dark at night to facilitate observations as well as keep any un-desirables away.

Meanwhile, about 30 miles out to sea and right off the coast the divers came in on, Submarine SSBN-728 slowly emerged. First the conning tower, then a pause while a lone sailer came out and using a handheld device, sampled the air and returned below, shutting the hatch as he did so. The sub stayed partially submerged and on station for about 30 minutes, then fully emerged and started to steam towards Port Canaveral. Several submariners emerged including the Captain. They took out large binoculars and scanned the sea for any signs of life, including birds or fish. The hand-held device the first crewman had was now permanently topside and plugged into the ship's network system. As the sailors scanned relentlessly, the Captain ordered an increase in speed.

"Keep a close watch for anything."

"Aye, Captain."

"Including debris of any kind, birds, fish, anything."

"Aye, Captain."

The Captain went below, as he did so radio and radar antennas deployed above the conning tower and the radar started to scan. Other antennas built into the hull of the tower tried to connect with satellites and other military channels. Nothing could be found. They scanned for activity on any band including aviation and heard nothing. As per procedure they monitored the guard channels, including the aviation emergency channel the airport tower divers were monitoring. Again as per procedure, the sub communications officers called out on these channels to announce their presence.

"Attention, attention, this is the nuclear submarine 'Persephone' off the Florida coast monitoring aviation and marine guard channels."

Back at the control tower, the divers looked at each other.

"Did you hear that?"

"I hear something, maybe the radio?"

The leapt to their feet and went over to the control panels and grabbed the microphone attached to the emergency frequency radio.

"Pan, pan.....pan pan, this is the crew of the dive boat 'Little Deeper' transmitting on the aviation emergency channel. Please repeat your message."

After about 15 second, a reply was heard.

"Little Deeper, Little Deeper, this is the submarine 'Persephone' calling on the aviation emergency channel, can we speak to the Captain?"

"This is Captain Hyatt, go ahead."

"Greetings Captain from the nuclear submarine 'Persephone,' can you tell me your location and condition of your crew and passengers?"

"Our location is at an airport tower in I believe the Melbourne Airport area. Crew and passengers are in good condition."

"This is the nuclear submarine 'Persephone,' thank you for the report. Are you able to travel north 15 miles to Port Canaveral?"

"We can do that."

"Our captain respectfully requests your company at the Navy docks at Port Canaveral. Do you have portable radio?"

"We have a portable marine radio and can monitor channel 16 for traffic. We need to discuss this plan with the crew and passengers, may we call you back in one hour?"

"Yes Captain, we will monitor this channel for your communications."

With that, the Captain put the microphone back on it's clip and looked at the others.

"Well, we are not alone and that's good. They probably have the equipment to figure out what has happened. Shall we go meet them?"

The others looked at each other and nodded in the affirmative.

"We can lock up this place in case we need to return, I found keys downstairs."

"Okay, if everyone is in, do we leave in the morning? Its going to be a long walk. The roads are not passible if we try to take an airport vehicle, so we are on foot."

"We are fine with that, the earlier we start the better, it gets hot here by mid day."

"Agreed. So lets clean this place up in case we need to return, pack all that you need in backpacks for a day's hike. It might be best to follow the beach as it leads directly to the sub base. There are lots of condos and hotels on the way we might be able to rest in if we need to. Maybe some water and dry food there as well. However assume the worst, bring enough water and food to make the complete journey. We need to get up and move out by 6 AM."

The divers and boat crew went to their individual areas and started preparing backpacks, which they had found while exploring what was left of the airport. There were a few desalinization straws to take along to get water from the ocean. Water bottles were gathered and attached to belts attached to the backpacks. Spare batteries for the marine hand-held radio were found and soon they were prepared enough to relax, sleep and get up early.

The following dawn, everyone was up and silently getting ready, very soon after that they looked up at the Captain and he said:

"Okay, lets go. Do a final check, make sure everything is off and remember to lock up.

They did their checks, shut off all of the power, walked down the steps, locked the door and went out into the cool air back towards the beach to commence the hike to the Cape. As they were not too heavily burdened with weight, the walked at a reasonable pace.

They made it to beach in good time, turned North and followed the arc of the waterline around to Cape Canaveral. 15 miles took most of the day with rest stops and food breaks, but the walk was generally easy as they could step in the water to keep cool and knew that many answers about their surroundings were waiting at the end of the Cape.

Along the way they again saw no activity. Periodically they would see fish carcasses and lots of seaweed filled with debris. Some buildings were destroyed. The newer ones with hurricane building code designs were still standing and looking reasonably well. At one point, they took shelter from the sun and went inside a condo's entrance area to both explore and maybe find a bit of food. They found the food, much of it rotting. They still did not find any people, which was very odd. Many of the doors were not locked, as if the inhabitants left very quickly. The other thing they noticed was that the ground floors of the condo they were in, had been completely flooded. The water must have risen at least 20 feet at one point, which would explain the massive amount of debris in the streets. Did the people have an early warning to leave quickly? Hopefully.

They marched along the beach for about six hours and then realized they were in reach of their goal. In another hour or so, they would reach their destination. Maybe the pace increased by a tiny bit. They were tired but hydrated, fed and anxious to find answers.

They rounded the tip of the Cape and found their way to Jetty Park, interestingly the sight of the very last Revolutionary War battle. The park was directly across the canal from the submarine base and the sub itself. Once they arrived the lookouts on the conning tower spotted them quickly and couple of dinghies were dispatched to pick up the divers and crew. The submariners checked them out thoroughly first and looked inside each backpack. Finding nothing, they allowed the group of people onto the boats and took them over to the sub to meet the Captain.

The sub was huge, an Ohio class at 560 feet long and 42 feet wide. Only about $1/5^{th}$ of it was above the water line. Nets were in place to allow them to move from the boats to the top of the sub, followed by an upward climb to the conning tower and then through a hatch. The Captain of the sub was waiting at the opening and greeted them as a group then as individuals.

"Welcome aboard the United States submarine Florida. Please follow me."

In single file they followed the Captain into the sub, down two flights of stairs and into a large meeting area which doubled as the galley.

"I imagine you're hungry and tired after your walk. There is plenty of food here so please grab some plates, find what you want and make yourself at home. We have a lot to talk about. I will return in 30 minutes."

The Captain left through some seriously respectful sailors standing at attention as he walked through on his way to the main control room. The divers and crew of the 'Little Deeper' immediately went for the food and water as it had been a long time since they ate properly. The galley crew from the submarine smiled at the activity. They helped dish out the food and motioned them over to a series of tables in the corner of the room where they ate well.

Exactly on time the submarine Captain returned with his executive officer. They sat down in front of the group and the Captain spoke:

"Ladies and gentlemen, we have a catastrophic situation here. Three days ago, the sun expelled a huge amount of highly charged particles from its interior. They formed a cloud of radioactive and extremely energetic protons and electrons that hit our atmosphere so hard it nearly ripped it off. The radiation was so intense that the majority of life on Earth was destroyed, much of it vaporized. The only survivors were those in deep mine shafts, underwater or in highly protected vaults. Our two groups were lucky enough to make it through this cataclysm however the struggle to survive might just be beginning. We do not have all of the information about the degree of radioactive contamination yet, we are talking to the others who are measuring our local environments as we are. It's best you all stay on board now as we can quickly get back to sea and get safely underwater. As you have probably have now figured out, water saved us all. It is the best defense against high radiation levels. As you may also know, while we were submerged there was major destructive weather on the land including thousands of tornados, winds in excess of 150 miles per hour, wild temperature fluctuations, spectacular auroras, earthquakes, tsunamis and just general rampage for about 48 hours. Most houses and any structures not designed to withstand hurricane force winds have been destroyed. The complete infrastructure of all nations has been destroyed as well. There is no electricity save the systems on board this and other submarines that were luckily out to sea. Water is scarce and possibly dangerous to drink on land. The air seems okay but there are still residual pockets of radioactive ionization in some areas; again it's best that you stay onboard until we know more about the situation. Finally, the magnetic poles have almost completely reversed due in part to the immense pressure of the solar wind on the Earth's magnetosphere. We expect the poles to stay reversed. So, that's all of the good news, the bad news is we need to find food and other people to survive. This submarine will keep us all alive for the next several months but not forever. Any questions?"

After a very long pause the 'Little Deeper's' Captain asked, "What can we do to help?"

"Quite a lot, I need you to monitor shortwave frequencies, document weather patterns, go out on search parties and in general become members of this crew. We run a tight ship and we need you to follow the regiment, order and guide lines for the safe operation of this vessel. This is a military ship and we run it with precision and discipline. I ask you to comply with all orders and help in any way you can. Will you do that?"

The divers and 'Little Deeper' crew nodded in the affirmative, clearly understanding that their lives had been saved and they needed to celebrate their great luck by becoming crew members of the sub.

For the next few weeks, they explored the surroundings, gathered what they could that would be useful and built a makeshift camp near the sub. At one point, a scouting party walked back to the control tower at the airport and retrieved a ham radio one of the divers had found in a truck. Even though the sub had shortwave communications capability the extra radio would come in handy. After returning, they would spend evenings outside listening to this radio in hopes that other people would try to communicate.

In fact they did hear voices on occasion, returned the call but heard no response. It was clear that there were others out there. The submarine Captain reported that they had heard other subs as well and interestingly, other dive teams. It seemed that anyone who was sufficiently under water survived. The sub Captains coordinated their searches as best they could and then decided to make their way to Port Canaveral. It had the best weather and had the best environment in terms of growing ability and low levels of radiation.

One by one, other subs showed up, not just American but Soviet, British and French. Europe and China also had central gathering spots where communications posts kept information flowing night and day.

Soon, Port Canaveral was filled with subs and they used nearby Kennedy Space Center as the new Capitol of the US. People who were in caves or deep shelters showed up from long walking treks to make a new city, albeit small one. Those who had purchased old missile silos in Colorado and Wyoming found their way over eventually. The airwaves started to get crowded with small groups every where.

After a year, they calculated that about 20 thousand people around the world were spared from the catastrophe, again mostly by way of protection by water.

On one nice evening, the divers from 'Little Deeper' and their crew decided to get together and have a camp fire on the beach. The crabs had to be shooed away and large turtles came out of the water periodically to lay eggs.

"The wildlife is coming back nicely."

"And the water and air, the streams and rivers around here are looking very clear."

"Want to hear something interesting?"

"Sure."

"I was doing some research the other day and the Mayans predicted that the poles would flip on the exact day that they did."

"Wasn't that prediction over a thousand years ago?"

"More like 1,200."

Silence followed as the people around the fire looked at the flames and watched the embers float into the sky and become stars for a moment.

MARS HIBERNATION

"I would like to die on Mars, Just not on impact." - *Elon Musk*

It had been a long wait, centuries in fact. A human being was actually going to walk on the planet Mars. Ever since Percival Lowell dreamt up ideas of life on Mars, people had wondered, some to abstraction, about how real it could be. Later, science took over and the idea of non confirmed life was distasteful and therefore we felt that until we knew for certain, life did not exist there. At some point late in the century, robotic probes and sophisticated computer simulations were able to present the possibility of life as real. The astrobiologi-

97

cal software programs took all of the realtime data and all of the known theoretical data and predicted (accurately by the way) the presence of life in some form on and in the planet. After the many decades of discussion, this fact did not come as a shock. What did come as a shock is the fact that the prediction and in situ measurements indicated a very strange type of life. One that would have unpredictable consequences when brought into contact with Earth life.

By committee of course, a decision was made to send a scientist to the planet for direct measurements. The habit of humans had been to send teams into space over the years but the danger was considered too great to take this chance. The space station would facilitate the mission by constructing a rocket capable of the trip and having the scientist depart and come back with this vessel.

The trip there and back would be long and tedious but the human factors specialist insisted that it was possible with new telepresence devices and continuous communications. They experimented with a few test subjects for up to a month in captivity and found that the idea was sound. The subjects transitioned into and out of the mock spacecraft in good mental condition. The telepresence devices made the experience as real as possible by projecting several people in the spacecraft at one time, all with interactive subroutines that included moods and general dispositions.

During this period of environmental design, the actual spacecraft was built in orbit. Robots, of course, took care of the majority of the work and a few astro/cosmonauts moved into the nearly finished craft for the final details and checkout.

The craft was deemed ready at about the same time a subject was chosen for the mission. The scientist, notable for his calm demeanor, was Owen Smith. He passed all of the psychological tests with ease and impressed all inquisitors. As almost an afterthought, they prepared him physically for the journey. The designers also took their time to explain how the journey would not be a lonely task as he would have several near-real team members to interact with. Although Owen was initially reluctant to have to interact with computer generated holographic projections, once he understood that each of the team members was modeled in great detail after the software engineers who created them, he felt more at ease. Personality profiles and psycho-social templates where programmed into the holograms. A self aware and autonomous main program structure assured very realistic interactions. The holograms even interacted with each other once they were all on board the spacecraft.

Once read and all of the paperwork signed, Owen boarded a shuttle and flew to the orbiting craft. Several others came with him to set up the last mission profiles and make sure that Owen was comfortable with his surroundings. He explored the corridors and looked in every room slowly to take it all in. At first he ignored the holograms and concentrated on the real components of the ship. The holograms did not understand this behavior and became a bit concerned. However this period did not last long as Owen had now convinced himself that the ship was sound and he felt comfortable to now deal with his shipmates.

"It actually feels quite comfortable once you get used to it," he mentioned to mission control, "as the projection details were vivid and almost real." A transition was eventually made where he interacted with these projections as if they were totally real. The feedback from these entities was the direct reaction to Owen's questions, comments and moods. Amazingly, the projections were strong enough to make the renderings solid in appearance. Low light levels helped as well as cameras near the viewer's position that facilitated the coordination of the image projections.

"Let's get this show on the road," proclaimed Owen, tired of waiting and practicing his mission. "You can teach me the rest while I am on my...on our way."

The designers by now felt comfortable with their work as well as Owen's state of preparation. They ran out of excuses to delay the trip and with one final go/no-go check around the room, started the count down.

Owen made his way to the cockpit and strapped in. The holograms took up their positions. The only real issue with them is that they could not physically move anything, like a switch or control handle. Instead they stood by the areas that would be controlled internally by the computers but to add to the realism, the holographic crew members would appear to be moving controls and throwing switches. This was really for Owen's benefit. Also for Owen's benefit was the fact that half of the crew members were females, some quite attractive. Instinctually, he smiled when he talked to them.

Within minutes the spacecraft was accelerating and changing direction, moving it out of Earth orbit and heading for the Red Planet. The g forces were mild but lasted for quite a long time. This was due to the nature of the propulsion in the spacecraft. Ion engines were being used that could work continuously for days and weeks if necessary. The only consequence was the lack of high g loads. In chemical rockets, these high accelerations lasted minutes but could place intense pressures on the astronauts and cosmonauts of the past. Modern propulsion was based on electric currents and highly accelerated gas particles. The ion Jet had recently been invented that could take any particles in space and accelerate them at velocities near the speed of light using only electricity. Therefore the spacecraft Owen was in, named *Persephone*, was covered with solar cells and had a resident nuclear reactor to generate the current necessary for the voyage.

Once in the cruise phase of the journey, life got down into a routine for Owen and his companions. Owen started to feel close to certain ones as their adaptive algorithms produced personalities that resonated with Owen's view of life. The other crew members seemed to be too serious or too argumentative and Owen judged them as he would any other human. He found himself spending more time with his "friends" as he and their programming found peace together. Owen knew that if one of them became intolerable, he could simply switch it off, unlike real people. He enjoyed the thought but never had to exercise the prerogative as the designers had included degrees of sensitivity in the programs, allowing for rapid and significant personality changes.

Weeks then months went by and most things went smoothly. The holograms operated flawlessly even when there were major radiation storms that forced Owen to seek shelter in the water-surrounded safety areas. He found it interesting that this fundamentally important substance, necessary for life, was also the one that would protect it from the major threat in space travel. He was almost jealous as he had to hide in his safe cocoon while the others went on with their business. The only real scare for Owen came when a projection power supply for one of his favorite female crew members malfunctioned and shut off the image periodically. Owen was so used to the interaction he genuinely felt fear of losing her. The issue was quickly resolved with a new power supply, but left an impression nonetheless.

Soon, the image of Mars was growing larger in the view screens and windows and the ship turned about to started to braking for orbital insertion.

Years before, the space agency had the foresight to send robots to Mars to build a structure suitable for human habitation. They had done their job admirably, using the local materials of water and sand to build bricks. The water was melted before it was mixed with the sand, then allowed to freeze again. Water was also used for the cement between bricks. At 50 below zero at night, ice can be quite strong. Walls were made, rooms and corridors were also made, exposed to the outside to keep their strength. Insulating materials were used to keep the future inhabitants comfortable and the walls strong. Many buildings had been built during this time and the rest of the electrical and plumbing components had been added. Owen would find many thousands of square feet of living space upon his arrival.

The craft found its way into orbit and settled for a few spins as the landing craft was readied to descend to the surface.

The landing would include a high speed atmospheric entry followed by braking from a ablative ballute system. The last portion of the landing would include the use of long, thin wings and finally thrusters for the last seconds of the touchdown.

Executed flawlessly, they settled onto the Martian surface, near the equator on what was a summer day for the planet. Temperatures here could get up to 80 degrees Fahrenheit but more typically around 30. Today was a very nice day and he got to experience 60 degrees for an hour or so after he opened the hatch and made his way into the shelter.

"*Nice outside*," thought Owen.

His holographic friends could not follow him outside but simply reappeared in the shelter and were waiting for him once he made it inside. He had chosen his favorites of course and left the more serious ones inside the ship to take care of the various spacecraft systems.

Once the door was latched shut, Owen made his way into the outfit room where he could shed his spacesuit, which was almost unnecessary in the warmth outside. The future for Mars would include the introduction of Earth plants and organisms that would take in the CO^2 and manufacture Oxygen. Within a generation, Martian air would be breathable with a small face mask to supplement the particular needs of the individual. The temperature would also rise due to this atmospheric manipulation.

Once the suit was off, he made his way to the control room where the holograms were now waiting for him.

"Hello everyone, how was the journey?" None of the projections understood the joke and simply looked at him. He shrugged and went on with his exploration of the facility.

"Looks nice, they did a fine job."

For the next several days, Owen checked out all of the life support systems, the greenhouse, the food preparation systems and of course the living quarters, which were ample and featured large windows to view the Martian landscape. He could see the dust storms and tornadoes dance across the surface. At night the stars were very bright as the atmosphere was about the same density as Earth's at 85,000 feet. This would be a great place for an observatory. The first one planned included components Owen had brought along. The idea was not to use one large reflector but a lot of smaller refractors. Each one would have an imager that could be used in conjunction with many other refractors to form a single picture of the cosmos. After Owen had set up the first array, the pictures he produced were amazing. With more refractors the image just got better and better.

The greenhouse was coming along and due to the low gravity, the plants were very large and ungainly. Many had reproduced by sending tendrils out. Many others needed help as there were no bees present (yet) to pollinate the plants. He would have to do a lot of work here for the next crop. One third of Earth's gravity felt pretty good and he could sprint around and easily jump ten feet in the air. This was a double-edged sword however, as he also had to work out at least one hour per day to keep his muscle tone up enough to return to Earth. Without this exercise, he would be doomed to stay on this planet forever. In fact, families who would eventually colonize the planet evolved into long thin people after just a few generations, just like we had perceived aliens to be.

Owen's job was to determine if life was on the Red Planet. He set about to determine this by traveling several miles away and looking at what seemed to be a melting pool of liquid that periodically came out of a mountain side. Spectroscopic analysis determined that it was indeed water but the question was, did it nourish life? Only close examination and sampling could determine the answer to this question. To that end he prepared a roving vehicle for the trip with sterile sampling equipment and provisions for at least a day. One of the holograms would come with him, the others could monitor from the base camp. He chose Zelda, his favorite as she was as attractive as she was affable. He took a long time to "pre-flight" the vehicle and make sure everything was in working order. It had been on the surface of Mars for many months without operating frequently. Soon, however, he was satisfied that it would be safe and sat down with the remaining holograms to make a mission plan. They worked for several hours making sure they had contingency plans for any problems that might occur. It was still risky to send the only human out on a mission like this as the remaining "crew" could not physically operate any equipment or open any doors.

The next day was launch day. Owen bid farewell to his holograms and entered the exploration vehicle for the long trip. Although the springs were only a few miles away, the drive would be slow and arduous as they had to navigate rough terrain and shifting sands. Robotic vehicles could have done some of the work but there is no substitute for humans when it comes to making decisions on the spot.

They departed and drove for several hours, managing not to get stuck in the sand by careful navigation. It was dusty and dirty out there. The wind blew at around 50 miles per hour but it felt like a gentle breeze due to the very thin atmosphere.

Once at the site, Owen entered his space suit, checked all of the systems thoroughly and depressurized the vehicle. Zelda remained in place, watching as he opened the access door and walked out onto the surface of Mars. Dust swirled as he do so and faintly followed him as he walked away towards the frozen springs.

The area where the springs emanated from was very nice in fact. It featured multi-colored rock formations, crystals, arroyo like sand swirls and faint, small pieces of...

"Life! There's life here! These pieces of dark vegetation look just like lichen in the frozen tundra of Earth's high altitude mountain areas!" Owen was ecstatic with the discovery, smiling broadly and looking for someone to share the excitement with.

"Zelda? Are you on frequency?"

"Yes, I hear you five by five."

"Zelda, are you in contact with the base camp?"

"Yes, we have a solid satellite link now and for the next 45 minutes."

"Relay the following words to base camp: Mars outpost Station One here, Owen Smith reporting. I have found life near a spring on the planet. It looks similar to high altitude lichen on Earth. I will be taking samples back to the laboratory for analysis. For now I am sending several pictures. Owen Smith out."

"The words have been sent, I will let you know when a confirmation is received."

"Good, thank you Zelda."

He took several pictures from different angles of the first outcropping of Martian Lichens, then took some samples and placed them in a Ziploc plastic bag. Next he made his way to the area where the water seemed to be coming from. It looked like a spring that came out of a rocky area, probably when the temperature was warm enough. Looking around, he noticed that the rocks in this general area were dark and would absorb heat. He thought about the climatology of this area of Mars and realized it could get quite warm (by Martian standards) during the summer. Ice formations could provide the necessary water for the winter months as the lichen seemed to be near areas where ice could form.

He walked around the area to perform a complete survey, taking pictures frequently and measuring temperature, humidity and taking air samples at various spots around the rock outcropping. As he moved to another vantage point, he did not realize that he was standing on a thin layer of dirt covering ice. He slipped and started to fall. This took place in slow motion, like the astronauts when they visited the Moon so long ago. As he rotated in space he also came down on a large rock with very sharp edges, possibly a crystal structure. One of the points tore into Owen's suit and ripped a hole at least a foot long just below his right arm and towards the midsection of his back. The pressurization was gone immediately and Owen's last memory was that of intense cold. By the time his body was rolling on the ground, his basic body functions were shutting down. He raised an arm in an attempt to move and simply froze in place. The telemetry from his suit sent confusing messages to Zelda.

"Owen, this is Zelda, do you copy?"

"Owen, this is Zelda, do you copy?"

"Owen, this is Zelda, do you copy?"

Zelda was powerless to help so she relayed a report back to base and asked for advice. The reply was to stay for another hour then return the vehicle.

An hour passed without any word from Owen, the suit telemetry had stopped as well. Zelda commanded the access hatch to close and activated the vehicle to return to home base. This trip was slower than the initial one, as computers had to make decisions about where to turn and how to avoid obstacles. The trip took almost four hours. When she was within 1000 feet, the local WiFi took over with much wider bandwidth and transferred her image back to within the base camp. The vehicle continued autonomously and finding the garage door, entered, parked and shut down.

The other holograms were unemotional about the loss of their captain. They were only capable of answering the queries from Earth with "Telemetry from the Captain is unavailable at this time."

As it takes so long to travel to Mars, the Earthbound scientists and engineers could only speculate about Owen's disposition. It would take months to determine what might have happened and years to plan a mission specifically to go back to the area of the stream`. As it seemed obvious that he had expired, an emergency situation was not at hand.

In actuality, five years passed before any other humans came to the outpost. When they did, most of the holograms had lost systems power and were no longer available. The outpost's main computers were in a very low level of activity, taking care of the most basic need; keeping the temperature regulated. The new visitors spent weeks bringing the equipment back into working order. They did this by replacing quite a lot it and fixing what they could.

At some point they had the time and interest to go and find out what happened to Owen. They had the basic position information for him as well as some supporting visual details from the last drive to the sight.

This time they used several vehicles with many humans inside. They had moved past the place where robots and holograms did most of the work. The trip, however, was still arduous as the local geology had changed very little in the intervening time.

What they found at the site of the springs was a combination of amazing and shocking. Owen's body was frozen in place within the shadow of a small outcropping, with his arm raised and the same expression on his face as when he spoke his last words. There was no damage to the body as the Carbon Dioxide and very low temperature in the shade conspired to freeze him quickly and thoroughly.

After due consideration, the team decided to keep him in this state while they returned his body to the outpost. They would seek guidance from the space agency on Earth. This process would ultimately take a month, not due to the propagation time between the planets but due to the time to make a decision on Earth.

It was decided to attempt to thaw Owen out, which came as a surprise to the astronauts at the outpost. The reasoning was that the air and temperature on Mars was optimal to suspend life without freezing the water within the human body; it would instead change to a thick fluid that slowly moved about. The theory was that Owen's heart still was working and beating at a rate of one pulse per hour. The low gravity contributed to minimize the effort required to do so. It was possible, therefore, that Owen was still alive.

They took him into a large laboratory at the base, lowered the temperature as much as they dared and prepared a chamber to slowly thaw out Owen. They placed him inside lying down on a table made of stainless steel. EEG, EKG and temperature probes were attached. The chamber door was shut and the process was initiated. Slowly the temperature was increased while the crew members monitored the sensors attached to Owen. As predicted, electrical activity started to increase as he warmed up. It was still surreal to observe, even after physicians at home felt confident about the outcome. The amount of activity accelerated as they approached the normal body temperature of 98.6. Twitching and gasps followed as the body was definitely waking up. At some point the video monitors showed Owen moving about and attempting to sit up. They called over a loud speaker and asked him to relax for a minutes as they stabilized the system and started to open the door to the chamber. Owen acknowledged the request, which indicated that his mind was capable of understanding language. He laid still until the door was opened and fresh air came into the chamber. They wheeled him out and carefully assisted him to sit up.

"How do you feel?"

"Its cold in here."

"Yes, it is. We are changing the thermostat now, so just relax."

"Okay....so....what happened?"

"From what we can tell, you slipped and ripped your suit open, then fell to the ground and were frozen almost instantly."

"How long have I been out?"

"Five years."

"Five years!?"

"Yes, Sir."

"Oh my goodness! Does my family know I am back with the living?"

"Not yet, but they will soon."

"Oh, my. Well this is a shock. A welcome one I guess. What has happened over the last five years? Why did it take so long to resuscitate me? What has my family been doing?"

"We will answer all of your questions soon, Owen. For now you need to rest and let your body adjust back to normal."

"Okay."

They helped him into a wheel chair and took him to a warmer part of the facility, where he could relax and start the process of catching up. Immediately he went to his computer and connected with the Internet. This was an internal version made just for the outpost but had semi recent news and information about home on Earth. As the people started to file out of his room, he noticed a very slight humming as they moved. When they touched something there seemed to be an increase in this sound. Although it was faint, it was still real. He watched and listened as they closed the door behind them but before the last one was out, she said:

"Get some rest. We will be back soon to check on you."

"Okay, thank you."

"Hmm. That's odd," he thought, "maybe I am a bit hazy."

He started his computer and began to search local news and emails regarding his family. It looked like quite a bit had transpired on Earth, more than he expected. World governments had signed a collaboration treaty that essentially opened all borders and established a single currency, which was only electronic. No paper or coins were to be made. There was a central government which made all announcements of importance pertaining to anywhere on Earth. Most if not all jobs were online and as a result of these changes, the quality of life in all impoverished areas was greatly improved. Most medical needs were taken care of tele-robotically or online only.

The more he researched the more he became concerned, as the videos of people looked somewhat different than what he remembered. People moved stiffly and did not seem to notice each other. His family had a lot of photos and details about their lives posted online. His wife had not remarried, his kids looked much the same but older. His parents looked the same and in fact exactly the same, which was also odd. Looking further he noticed that funeral notices and birth announcements were nowhere to be found. What had happened?

During his research, the astronauts at the outpost would check in on him. They were friendly and concerned but still came and went with that faint buzzing sound. He answered their questions and endured their tests, but really wanted them to leave so he could return to his research. Once they had gone, he made more discoveries that concerned him. Communications were transmitted solely by the Internet, which had grown immensely in size and capabilities. The oceans were strewn with fiber optic cables, satellites were only used for deep space missions and power was completely supplied by solar or wind, although the wind generators, being mechanical, were being replaced with non-mechanical pressure-sensitive designs. The Earth was becoming very quiet. People did not fly anymore, ships were completely robotic and all of the cars had been parked. There was no interest in travel.

Then it came to him, about the faint buzzing. In his youth he noticed that when whole neighborhoods lost power, from a storm or electrical problem, there was an uncanny silence. Also, when on a boat an out at sea, the same silence found him; he realized that the humming of AC current actually moved the devices it was powering in a very subtle way but just enough to set the background noise level. So too was he experiencing this noise level when the astronauts were present at the outpost. He began to suspect that they were not entirely human. The odd changes in Earth life was another hint.

When they returned to check up on him he asked:

"How long did you say I have been in hibernation?"

"Five years, Sir."

"Are you sure?"

"Why do you ask?"

"I am concerned that so much has changed over just five years. The Earth is much different but my family looks about the same, especially my parents. I am also wondering if you people are entirely human. What is really happening?"

"All in good time, Sir."

"No, I need to know now."

"We are trying not to upset you, we need you to relax first."

"Upset me about what?"

"We are concerned that so much has changed while you were preserved that it will be too much of a shock to understand all at once."

"Okay then, lets start with the basics."

"Well, Sir, you have not been frozen for five years, its actually been 500 years."

"Oh my, I was concerned about the time, just not that much. What about my family, the dates on the computers, the Internet?

"We control all that you have seen on the computers."

"What about my family?"

"They are doing quite well and look about the same as when you were frozen."

"I see. So they have lived for over 500 years?"

"Yes, and they will live quite a bit longer than that."

"How is that possible?"

"Humans are now hybrids."

"Of what?"

"Biologicals and Silicon."

"How so?"

"Medical research long ago discovered the ability to modify the DNA during its reproductive cycle; normally the telomeres on the DNA strands hold the blueprint for the replication of the cells. We discovered how to perfect that process, ostensibly to fight cancers and other debilitating diseases. We found that if we allowed for a full spectrum approach to cell reproduction, in other words, allowing each cell in our bodies to replicate perfectly, we would live forever. In the early 21st century several secret laboratories worked on this process and within a few years, thousands of 'perfects' were made. Within another hundred years the 'perfects' were integrated with silicon to allow direct connection with the Internet and each other."

"Wow, so you're a combination of analog and digital?"

"A crude way of describing it, but yes."

"What about the resulting population explosion?"

"Most people have been sent out to the stars to colonize their planets. Being 'perfect' also allows us to combat radiation sickness to a great degree. Radiation causes cancer, our process eliminates cancer cells, therefore we can go to the stars without concern. Also, and partly based on what you have just gone through, we discovered that our process lends itself nicely to hibernation. Any residual problems after re-awakening is taken care of with the Process."

"The Process?"

"That is what we call the medical procedure that is now performed on all adults once they have matured. They ostensibly are held at that age forever. Once several years have passed, they probably will be chosen for spaceflight. Earth now has a very low population; there is really no reason to stay there, when there is so much more to discover."

"I'll bet the animals and aborigines liked that."

"Indeed, they now are taking over."

"So, what about the silicon? You said you were now integrated with it, can you explain that to me?"

"At maturity, we implant a silicon node into a person. Its much like what you know of as an integrated circuit but very much more advanced. It includes meta-materials and quantum computers linked directly to antenna arrays. The node is always in the 'background' mode where a person is not consciously aware of it but can evoke its operation at anytime. Most people use it as a backup to memory and a tool to perform complex processes. Nodes connect to each other in a web-like network and they connect to what you once knew as the Internet and finally to the chronosynclastic infundibulum."

"And what's that?"

"A point in space where a person's existence in space-time ceases to be linear and becomes discrete. A person that has entered the chronosynclastic infundibulum exists at multiple points and lines in space-time. This person exists at all points in time in one place and can also appear at many other places at the same time. This is due to the network topology we have designed into the web. If I need to check on my sibling or offspring, I simply move to their 'address' and start experiencing what they are experiencing."

"Oh my, that's in a way amazing and in a way frightening."

"How so?"

"No peace and no solitude."

"There is nothing but peace now, no one has been killed by war, aggression or accident for hundreds of years. Anyone who has violent thoughts is reprogrammed. As far as solitude, you can be as far away from the web as you want mentally, just do not evoke it's connection."

"And what about creativity?"

"Enhanced, as you can quickly discover how unique your thoughts really are."

"But can't someone watch you being creative and take your ideas?"

"Yes, but you have the first time stamp and will prevail."

"Okay, and what about work? What do people do for a living?"

"There is no work, per se. All physical work is done by robots. People design, engineer, explore, create and have their ideas brought to fruition by the robots and automatons."

"That's very cool except that there are people who are only capable of physical work and do not have the mental facilities to design or engineer."

"Those people are no longer with us."

"Where did they go?"

"They died natural deaths."

"So they did not undergo the 'process'?"

"No."

"Did they have a choice?"

"Yes, but most did not take that option, choosing instead to live out their lives naturally."

"Hmmm, okay."

"Discovery and engineering was stressful to them, some of them chose to be artists but most chose to stay behind."

"I see. Well I have much to learn from this new world. For now, however, I need to know what is to become of me?"

"You will be given the option to undergo the 'process' as your genetic structure and biology is severely compromised from your time on this planet.

"Okay, do I have to undergo the 'process' as well as the implant?"

"It is highly recommended that you do so."

"Why? I am not sure I wanted to be a node."

"Then you will be like a plant at the bottom of a shallow lagoon. Life will appear to ebb and flow in front of you without rhyme or reason as you see the water with its inhabitants move about seemingly in a random fashion. You will not be able to keep up to the advancements we are experiencing and soon you will be in a constant state of confusion. You will exist in this state forevermore."

"I see. Okay I would like to think about this a bit more before I make a decision."

"We understand. Remember that your body is in poor shape and needs attention immediately, please make your decision as soon as you feel comfortable."

"Okay."

At this point, he rose and decided that the best course of action was to go for a long walk to consider the positives and negatives of his new world and whether or not to join it. Although weak, he walked through the greenhouse, which always gave him peace. He sat for a while inside, then ventured to the control rooms and laboratories. He realized as he did so that the people at the station normally just moved about and spent very little time in one place. They were like dolphins, moving about constantly, ever curious and stopping periodically to take a breath. These people did much the same without the stopping. They moved their gaze to and fro with an occasional stop to examine something in particular, then they were off walking again. Owen fell into the rhythm and followed several around for a while. He knew the exercise was good for them and also realized they could be connected to machines far away creating things that interested them. He watched and thought about what had been left behind, which at this point, was stored in a memory bank at a server farm.

Then there was the matter of his family; they had all been 'processed.' What he could go back to certainly would be not what he left. They would be polite and move on mentally as he would not be at their level without conversion.

What else was on Earth now? Were there groups of people in the hills that refused to convert? His recent conversation on the subject led him to believe the aborigines or natives had chosen to remain as they were. However they were living with masses of geniuses who in essence controlled them. Was this a paradise for the natives?

"Probably not," he thought out loud.

It was a severed society, with an ever-increasing gulf between their self interests. If the geniuses eventually left, the natives would inherit a world devoid of overpopulation and with a recovering ecosystem. Flora and fauna could return to their old levels. Animals in zoos could be released. Hopefully the errors of the past would not be repeated.

"Hmmm."

On the other hand, the discovery of the Universe would take on a much faster pace if he joined the geniuses. They had already begun to fly to the stars and their associated planets. So many had been found that it was extremely rare to find a star without planets. Stirring up a cup of coffee creates a central mass in rotation with concomitant eddies at different radii from the center. This is simply how nature works. The speed of rotation and the density of the material dictates how many planets and at what distances from the star are formed.

What a great experience to be able to see and understand the nature of the Universe and the life it contains.

Then of course, he could be one with his family.

"I need to sleep on this."

He found his way back to the control room, determined where his quarters were and proceed there. Once inside, he shut the door, found the bed and giving in to his exhaustion, fell deeply asleep.

His dreams were bizarre, rampant and at times intense. There were images of water, streams, dust, cold, people, machines and computers that morphed from their impersonal states to having faces and voices. The computers looked and talked to him all at once.

He awoke several times that night, usually startled. He was cold one moment and hot the next.

After a fitful night, he awoke late the next morning feeling mentally bruised with residual feelings of anxiety and exhaustion. He sat on the side of the bed for a long time before he could command his body to stand. He was stiff and sore from the hibernation and after effects of the lousy night's sleep.

"Good morning," he heard from an intercom speaker in his room.

"Maybe.....hopefully."

"Did you have a restful evening?"

"No, not really."

"Well, the rest of us did, if you join us you too will sleep well."

"Yeah, I understand but I will not make such an important decision quickly."

"Of course."

Owen spent the rest of that day considering his options. Should he play God? Should he undergo the 'Process' and join his family and friends in an elite automatous society? Or should he live the rest of his life out naturally on Earth, watching the wildlife return and the elite leave?

At some point he realized that he did not want to be left alone and that he could always return to Earth many years from now to see the results of his other option. He walked over to the laboratory, found the person he had been dealing with and told him of his decision.

"I have decided to join your new society."

"Good choice, we have the equipment here and can perform the 'process' whenever you are ready."

"I'm ready now."

"Okay, I will assemble the team and meet you in the infirmary at five this evening."

"Perfect, I will see you there, thanks."

"You're welcome."

His last hours as a mortal were taken up in contemplation. He wondered how the balance of truth, belief and sensibilities would be disturbed. By watching the others he could tell they were much less emotional, all business and driven towards goals. They were a bit machine-like.

He went to the outpost kitchen for his last mortal meal. Tea, a sandwich and a piece of cake. Looking around, he noticed that the others seemed much more health conscious, not that it was bad to do so, just unimaginative.

After his lunch he rose, cleaned his area of dishes and went for a walk.

He thought, "What do geniuses see? Do their minds wander or stay in one place? Do they compartmentalize their mental efforts? Are they not interested in romance except when it's the right time to do so?

The amount of thinking about the pros and cons was tiring. Owen decided to calm down a bit and simply drink in the surroundings, hoping that they would not change tomorrow. With his mind running in idle mode, he smiled for the first time as he realized he had been brought back from the dead and should feel elated. He did, actually, but just had not had the time to feel the proper emotions.

"So what if I have to go to the next level of human existence, at least I am alive and in addition have this amazing opportunity," he thought.

He was feeling better about his decision to move forward now. He smiled yet again and sat back to feel the comfort of the chair he was sitting in.

Meanwhile, the others still moved about with subtle conviction. Owen watched them with slight amusement but caught something about their motions that was rather interesting. He watched for a bit longer then rose out of his comfortable seat to make sure he was really understanding what was happening. The only way to verify his observation was to carefully follow one of the others.

These people performed "rounds" much like doctors do in hospitals; they move from one task to another and seemed to repeat the same sequence over and over.

Owen followed one of the team members from a safe distance and noticed that she took care of one task then moved to another assigned task, concentrated on that one, then moved to another. Normally this would not be that different than other human activities however the whole process had a geometry to it. They did not spiral in like a Fibonacci series, they actually performed their tasks in circles. Owen changed personnel and followed another; he walked in a basic circle around the laboratories within the main building just like she did. He followed yet another and same thing! Each circle was of a different average diameter. More interestingly, the circles were performed clockwise around the center of the complex.

"Huh, thats amazing," he thought to himself, "Does this mean that I will walk in circles as well?"

And why circles? Was it the most efficient of forms? Would they move in concentric spheres without gravity?

He surmised that it was a matter of efficiency. They were of course, still all connected in the web, so they knew each other's activities and intentions. The circles kept them from bumping into each other, like driving lanes, so that was efficient as well.

He watched more people and their actions, then saw one going the opposite way, counter-clockwise.

"A lefty!"

She still had a clear lane though and still performed tasks without problems.

"Ingenious!"

Well, that was what he had to look forward to tomorrow, efficiency, focus and long life. Not too bad, huh?

Well maybe.

The appointed time came up quickly and he found his way to the medical complex to begin his transformation. Several medical staff were waiting for him when he arrived. They were courteous and professional.

"We will put you under for a few hours, then we will revive you slowly and begin the process of acclimating you to your new capabilities."

"Okay, when do we begin?"

"Right now, please lay down on the bed here, we will insert a tap into your vein and place a sensor cap on your head. Once you are out, we will insert a module into your neck and laser suture it closed, you will have no scar or sense that it is there. The module will deploy filaments that are self guided to specific parts of your cerebral cortex. Within about a week, you will sense the web and soon your mental powers will grow. At the same time your DNA will be rewritten to allow you to live quite a long time."

While they were discussing the details, a nurse deftly inserted the tap into his left arm and placed a comfortable cap with a wire bundle attached to his head. He laid down and soon felt drowsy."

"Please count down from 10."

Someone threw a switch on a panel to his left.

"How quaint, still doing a countdown?"

"It has worked for centuries."

"Well, how about if I count up instead? Does that sssssstilll........."

He was out cold now. They quickly cleaned his neck and after opening a slit a few centimeters long, inserted a small module, much like a large pill, inside. Within minutes, they were using a laser suture to close the wound. They placed disinfectant around the local area and attached a small bandaid. Backing up from their work, the doctor and nurses observed their accomplishment and called for a gurney to take Owen back to his quarters to sleep off the anesthetic.

The "pill" started its work immediately as did the nanorobots that were injected into his bloodstream. Even while he slept his DNA was being modified and neural connections were being established. He dreamt of crowded rooms and noise.

Within a few hours Owen started to stir. He moved his arm up to his head and rubbed his eyes. He felt very groggy and had the sensation of music being played in the background. Slowly he sat up, using his hands and arms to steady himself. A few seconds after he set up the nurse appeared.

"I see you are awake. How do you feel?"

"Like there are twenty people in my head, lots of noise."

"That will pass as your neural connections are starting to fuse. The whole process will take a while but in the end you will feel refreshed, have new energy and a positive outlook on life."

"Nice to hear, but now its pandemonium in my brain."

"Just relax, have some water and get your strength back. In a few hours we are going to get you up and walking."

"Okay, thanks."

A few hours later, Owen was lifted up by a few people which was made easy due to the Martian gravity. He was then assisted as he walked through the halls to regain his balance as well as his stamina.

A few hours later still he was on his own and exploring. The only remnants of the procedure was a small module on his belt which monitored his primary condition and sent the data to the doctors. Soon even that would not be necessary.

Now he understood the concentric walking, as he was left handed, he walked counter clockwise, much like running on a track or racing a horse. It was a lot more efficient, moving from area to area to do work or monitor progress. His mind was much stronger, even in these early stages of redevelopment. He felt good, he felt confident and could just start to understand how so many un-changed people wasted most of their lives.

"Pity."

He remembered the movie "*Charly*," adapted from the book '*Flowers for Algernon*,' where a mouse and then a mentally-delayed man were given treatments that tripled their IQs. Owen was starting to feel these effects, so many things were clear to him now and he could remember significantly more details than ever before. It was so easy to think, to explore, to create. Philosophy, astronomy, physics and biology were all so interrelated that they evolved in similar ways with similar structures. It was a dance of mathematics, poetry and life. He felt full of energy.

Then he started to hear voices and see images like projections from other people's eyes. The voices were monotonous and the visions un-unique, almost black and white. As time went by the visions and voices multiplied. So too did the ability to be part of the Internet, or maybe more accurately, the cosmic consciousness. He could just start thinking about a historical event for instance, and the details would come to him. It was like flying through history, circling when something caught his interest, changing altitude when he wanted to 'zoom in' or 'zoom out' for instance to see the effects of a small incident on the world surrounding it. Time flows like a river but it is undulated by other forces like gravity. Intense historical events moved at a different pace than the boring moments. There was oscillation, resonance, attraction, repulsion and peace. But peace is where you found it as all things are in constant motion, whether at a sub-atomic level or a galactic level.

He understood so much now and felt compelled to get in motion with the others; there was just too much to experience to just sit around. He joined the others and started running.

TIME TRAVEL

"The bottom line is that time travel is allowed by the laws of physics." - *Brian Green*

But it took a philosopher to figure out how time travel was to be achieved. As philosophy is the trunk of the knowledge tree, it was appropriate to have someone with access to all of the disciplines to finally understand how manipulating time could be done.

Physicists long ago assumed time was linear and that although it might move at different rates, time was ultimately defined as the distance between moments. They were perplexed at how to move forward or backward along this path.

The math was difficult as it was easier going forward as you could preserve yourself for a period of time and then come out to see what the future was like. Going backwards was more of a problem as there was no obvious recording of time to rewind.

A solution was found, however, when the philosopher reasoned that *if* within the next many millions of years time travel back into history is possible, then the existence of visitors now is possible. In fact, visitors from the future would certainly be interested in major events as we live them now. So if they are (or were) here, why can't we see them? Because they are nowhere to be seen. In fact the solution is to not be made of matter, only energy. Therefore the way to travel back in time is to replicate the electromagnetic conditions at the particular moment of interest, then observe it using virtual reality equipment. The solution came sooner than expected, in 2054. The conditions had to be replicated at the atomic level with a hadron particle accelerator and extensive computing power. Moore's law had kept true and the amount of energy and computational power needed to create the effect was available.

They tried small things at first, making subtle changes in archeological artifacts, like adding a small scratch or fleck of paint, just enough so the scientists of that era would not notice. They would go to the museums after their experiments and observe the changes.

Next they tried altering small bits of history by modifying words in letters and emails by subtle amounts and observing the change in history books.

Finally, it became obvious that observing things through someone else's eyes was possible and the least obvious way of going back in time. The trick was to be able to move the fields around as the subject moved around. Initial tests showed this to be a challenge and they kept losing lock with the image.

Finally good engineering prevailed and the tracking system worked to perfection.

One of the more interesting adjustments that needed to be accomplished was compensating for gravity, as the Earth grows by small amounts every year due to micrometeorites and space dust. The speed of time is directly proportional to the amount of gravity in the local reference plane. This means, as Einstein noted, that time moves faster when it has less gravity around it. This is why the Apollo astronauts of the '60s and '70s actually lived a few seconds longer than they would have when they returned to Earth.

Once their system was designed and tested properly, the scientists were able to send someone back to experience the past first hand. The first that went could only view the images from the host as they saw them. This was more like watching a movie, however even these first attempts found numerous mistakes on how history was recorded. The scientists chose people associated with famous personalities and famous events. Clearly the past had been recorded improperly in many cases, intentionally for some political or financial advantage at the time. In other cases, history was filled in when the scientists could view the events that were not recorded or where recordings were lost. The burning of the Library of Alexandria was one of the initial places they went. The findings were extraordinary and had the documents in that library survived, they would have had profound impacts on the centuries that followed.

A large academic team was formed quickly to compartmentalize the historical research and dedicated personnel were assigned specific tasks and assigned priorities. The time machine was busy 24 hours a day as a result.

Some thought was given to less structured research, and this is where Kieren was assigned to follow the life of an individual born in New York City in 1954. They picked carefully, someone who had led a unique life-one with proximity to several great people and events. This person was mobile and exploratory, they were not interested in anyone who was sedentary.

The equipment was prepared by tuning and setting the time period for when the subject was four years old and living in New York City with his parents. Kieren was only able to observe at this point, though later in the subject's life he might be able to make his presence known.

As it turns out, the team chose Kieren to relive his own life.

Kieren woke up and stood up in his bed, his mother Noreen came in to get him and took him to his breakfast. She was an actress on and off Broadway in New York and had studied at the Stanislovski acting school along with several notable actors who made many movies and TV shows. This included Kevin McCarthy and Peter Falk. Eventually, she would be in the very first play ever broadcast on TV.

His father, Donald was waiting and looked very happy to see him. His parents talked to each other as well as to the subject. Donald was a merchant mariner and part time student at the New School for Social Research. This school was comprised of mostly German refugees who had fled Germany at the rise of the Nazi party. Mostly social scientists and scholars, these professors made the school a very unique and important place as the quality of education was extremely high. These professors had led the way in social thought and progress over the first third of the 20th century. Donald and his brother Jack attended and eventually obtained their bachelors degrees. Donald, or Don, also spent quite a lot of time at sea, having started his Atlantic crossing in 1945 at the very end of the second world war. Reconstruction was in full swing however on his first voyages and he witnessed the massive destruction this conflict had brought to Europe including still burning ship's

127

hulks at certain harbors. The ship Don was almost exclusively on was called a Liberty ship, made in vast quantities to supply England and other parts of Europe. They were simple, about 440 feet long with a steam piston engine comprising a high, mid and low-pressure piston system fed by two boilers. The ship could make about 11 knots at sea which made a typical crossing from New York to England take about seven to eight days. They took bulk freight, pipes, machinery and general equipment across to rebuild nations. The smoke was just clearing from the war when he started and even 15 sailing years later those nations still needed significant amounts of supplies. He sailed from about six months then went to school for about six months. Also, during that time, he played jazz piano in New York. This was during the late 40s and 50s when a significant confluence of art, music and intellectual activity was transpiring. Legends in the fields of music, literature, painting and other social endeavors all came from this period. Don opened up famous jazz spots as well as played with some of the best musicians in that era. Times were also turbulent where the introduction of recreational drugs combined with new drinking privileges made for some people living some very wild lives. So wild in fact, that Don and Noreen were very concerned about bring up a child in the midst of this craziness. They frequently woke up with people asleep on the stairway going up to their loft.

Kieren witnessed, over the course of several months, the tumultuous nature of life with his parents, the amazing talents of those around them and the changing of the political climate in the nation in general. The Cold War was upon them, the newspapers and other news outlets talked about the arms build up and the tension between the Soviet Union and the United States. Spying activities were at an all time high, warships and advanced Air Force aircraft were being built at a prodigious rate. The consequences of this activity, although not understood at the time, was an economic focus on the military for both nations and the creation of new technologies originally made to cause destruction but ultimately to allow humans to venture to the stars. Before there were rocket ships, there were Intercontinental Ballistic Missiles.

During this period, Kieren saw his mother play Shakespeare in Central Park and his father open up the Five Spot Jazz cafe, which turned out to be a very important meeting place for artists and intellectuals alike. The following was reported in the history books decades after these events:

"The bar also attracted some neighborhood musicians, including a pianist and merchant marine named Don Shoemaker. When Shoemaker wasn't at sea, he organized jam sessions in his upstairs studio at 1 Cooper Square, next door to the bar. "They'd be coming down and buying a pitcher, a beer or whatever," Joe Termini (the owner) recalled. "They were running up and down and all that so Don Shoemaker says to me, 'Why don't you get a piano and we'll come play here." The Terminis liked the idea, so they purchased an old upright and applied for a cabaret license. They received the license August 30, 1956, and a week later opened for business as the Five Spot, the newest jazz club in Greenwich village. Shoemaker and a bass trumpet player named William Dale Wales simply moved the jam sessions downstairs and invited their friends to play. Within weeks of the club's reincarnation, the Five Spot earned a reputation as *the* local place for cheap beer and good music.

Painter Herman Cherry and sculptor David Smith were among the first wave of artist-regulars. The couldn't resist the music, or the seventy-five-cent pitchers of beer. They told their friends about the place, and soon the little bar became a coveted gathering spot for New York artists. The regulars included painters Willem de Kooning, Franz Kline, Joan Mitchel, Alfred Leslie, Larry Rivers, Grace Hartigan, Jack

Tworkov, Mike Goldberg, Roy Newell, Howard Kanovitz and writers Jack Kerouac, Ted Joans, Gregory Corso, Allen Ginsberg, Frank O'Hara, among others."

What followed was a list of jazz greats- Thelonious Monk, Charlie Parker, Dizzie Gillespie, Miles Davis and numerous others. Most of these people made numerous recordings and some overdosed on drugs causing great concern for the Shoemakers.

Don and Noreen eventually had to take their baby Kieren out of that city and into the opposite place in the Universe as far as progressive thought, El Paso, Texas. It was a shock for the whole family, except for maybe Kieren who was too young to understand the relevance of great change.

The adjustment for his parents was arduous but not without success. Don continued his schooling and earned a Master's degree in Political Science from Texas Western College. He also played jazz in local venues, gathering up local talented musicians hungry for the new style of music. Noreen found her way into local theatre, eventually taking over the lead roles for all of the most important plays that were performed locally. At the University, she performed Greek tragedies, existential dramas and plays like Under Milkwood, Lysistrata, Trojan Women, The Rivalry, The Women, Night of the Iguana, Irma la Duece and Mother Courage. In a way they led a cultural revolution in this part of Texas. As a result they were treated with respect and found themselves in the local papers frequently.

Meanwhile, Kieren was still observing through himself as a child, recording all he witnessed and finding the best opportunity to interact with the time line. But what temporal point would be the most useful area to adjust, and for what purpose? The team decided to make a subtle change during Kieren's adolescence. This was at a point when daydreams were as close to real as life itself; where the clarity of these dreams was both fungible and had the most impact on the senses. Dreaming about spaceflight led for instance to the creation of a trans-atmospheric vessel that could be used many times to shuttle equipment, people and technology to space stations and orbits high above the Earth. This concept was beyond science fiction at the time, however as science fiction steers our tasks in the future in so many ways, the team decided to make a suggestion that young Kieren would carry into his adult life and act upon.

While he was drawing one day and completely lost in a day dream about flying around the stars, Kieren started to shape a main vehicle with wings that could glide to a landing. Because fuel was so heavy, he fashioned a large expendable tank to his vehicle that would detach when empty. He also added two solid rockets to the sides of this assembly to quickly get heavy loads off of the launch pads. The inputs from the team came from a phalanx of mechanical, electrical and aerospace engineers. The results were simple drawings and a memory implant of why it was such a good design.

He grew up to live a life of science and wonderment. He became a radio astronomer and was able to listen to Jupiter-like planets in star systems relatively close to our own. He surmised correctly that even though thousands of planets had been discovered in the "Goldilocks zone," a place of moderate temperatures and size, it took Jupiter-like outer planets in these systems to sweep out the errant asteroids, comets and meteors that could set back the development of life in these candidate planets.

The creativity of his parents gave him the genes to move science ahead just a little bit.

Kieren, years later, worked at NASA and became part of the design team that was responsible for following up the success of the Apollo Moon missions.

From that, the time travelers were able to witness the change almost first hand. They could see the cultural, emotional and phenomenological connections from the past to the present and put real time life in the proper perspective.

At some point on a hot, humid day in Houston, Texas he leaned forward and said:

"I've got an idea....."

CLONES NOW

"Human Cloning is Coming" - *Mike Pence, Governor of Indiana*

Whenever there are dogs that have unusually good smelling capabilities, and work for border patrol, they get cloned. Although there are a great many dogs with special capabilities, what I am talking about is dogs within species that excel. These dogs are the best of the best, the 1% of the 1%, and these are chosen to be copied. This practice started in the 1990s and persists today. As a result the agencies interested in this type of talent have dogs which are genetically superior than the rest. Generations of these dogs have come and gone, the technique is well practiced and well understood. It keeps us safe, as on well over 100 cases, these special dogs have detected explosives attempted to be smuggled or nerve agents or extremely harmful biological agents.

Miami airport 1990

Jessup made his way down the jetway and onto the corridors that led to immigration and border patrol. It had been a long flight from Sao Paulo but he was glad to be home and looking forward to re-uniting with his family. He walked with the rest of the passengers and eventually came up to an opening with a significant number of uniformed personnel. People with U.S. passports to the left and all others to the right. He bore left and queued up with the rest for the first step of coming back home. Eventually he was next in line, standing ten feet away from the agent in the glass booth. The agent looked up an motioned for Jessup to come forward.

"Passport?"

"Here you go, Sir."

The agent checked the passport number, flipped through the pages and after the computer screen gave him the okay, stamped one of the pages and looked up.

"Welcome back." He handed the passport to Jessup.

"Thank you, its nice to be home."

Now onto immigration and a baggage check. Down another corridor he went and to a moving baggage system which had stopped motion and held a multitude of bags. He spied his luggage and after retrieving it, made his way to an inspection area.

"Place your bags on the floor here," said a guard.

The passengers complied and placed their bags in a random array on the floor. Another guard appeared with a small Cocker Spaniel and walked briskly from bag to bag. The dog wagged its tail and smelled each one quickly. Within a few minutes the dog was done and led back to a room presumably to wait for the next crowd. The dog looked totally harmless and appeared to be having fun.

"Amazing," thought Jessup. "in this technologically sophisticated era we still rely on dogs to keep us safe."

The dog, "Trixie" by name was led back to a small room with a few other dogs and immediately went over to a small bed to lay down. It spun around a few times, curled up and put its head down to relax. The trainer looked down at it.

"Best nose we ever had."

"Yep," said a guard standing nearby. "Definitely the best."

"I think she could qualify for the 'Dolly' program."

"What's that?"

"A new program to breed the best dogs so we can get the best noses."

"Hmm, makes sense."

They looked down the now sleeping dog and smiled, not knowing that the "Dolly" program was not exactly a breeding program.

Later that month, Trixie had an appointment with a vet panel to determine if she was indeed qualified for the "Dolly" program. She was examined thoroughly and deemed healthy, then tested carefully to determine the extent of her smelling abilities. They brought smaller and smaller amounts of explosive residue until she was unable to discern the odor. Her sensitivity was exemplary. They tried small amounts of various compounds, each with a small portion of explosive residue. She was deemed unusually sensitive and in fact able to discriminate many different aromas with astonishing accuracy.

"Definitely a good candidate," the vet board reported. They quickly signed the necessary documents that started to process to get the dog into the program. Within a week she had been transferred to Plum Island, just off of Long Island. This by the way was the venue for a significant amount of sensitive research in biological agents in the 1960s. They had extensive medical facilities and a very competent staff. Interestingly not only did they have veterinarians, but they also had genetic scientists, stochastic theoreticians and biologists specialized in incubations.

The dog went in without its trainer, which stressed them both. Soon the dog was anesthetized and several bio-samples taken. In a few hours she was waking up from a foggy slumber and stumbling to walk. An hour after that she was completely normal with just a few tiny pains from the incisions. She licked them instinctively.

Within days the samples (or Trixie 2) were in the incubation facilities and headed for a special growing chamber that could replicate a dog's womb. Trixie 1 was sent home a week later to her waiting trainer. She served out her career in an exemplary manor and was retired to live out her life in a nice suburban home with her master. Even near death she could still raise her head and look in the direction of an interesting smell. Clearly her stereo nose worked until the end. Her master, still working, took an assignment to train with another dog. This would not be the last time he interacted with his beloved dog, though.

After Trixie 1 had expired, the master was working with another dog and had the opportunity to change work areas to another airport. He showed up for his first day there an hour early to get his new dog acclimated and relaxed with the new venue. They walked the halls and examination areas, careful not to get the other dogs distracted. As they were doing this, the master had a "deja' vu" moment as he saw another dog in the distance which looked very much like his old dog Trixie. He looked for a long while but dismissed the idea as just an illusion, probably from his fond memories of his old partner. They walked towards another area and soon returned to the main office to get assigned a baggage carousel area where passengers picked up their luggage from foreign flights. Soon they were working and screening bags at a high rate of speed. The new dog was good, but not stellar.

Hours later as the had worked pretty much straight through on many hundreds of bags, the master looked up and saw the Trixie look-alike once again. But this time she was much closer. He looked for a bit longer and noticed the new dog was losing concentration on her tasks, much to the annoyance of her master. The dog had raised its head and was sniffing at the air while wagging her tail. The master was clearly upset and started pulling her leash back towards the bags. The dog resisted and was being pulled while sliding her feet. She was clearly agitated about something. Then she saw the master of the old Trixie and immediately started running in place while sliding to try to get to him. The dog trainer was clearly annoyed but had no choice but to let the dog go over to the other pair. As the look-alike got closer she was whimpering and clamoring to get closer, using all of her energy to do so. Once they got even closer she rose up on her back legs and pawed the air. The original Trixie master was stunned as she looked in every detail like his old dog. She also acted exactly like the original Trixie and appeared to recognize the old master. Then at close range she licked him and whimpered and acted like she had not seen him in years. It was a magical experience for both of them but more confusing for the master as he did not understand why this dog was so excited and so much like his old Trixie.

Once the excitement died down, he had a chance to talk to the other trainer.

"This is amazing," said the master, "this dog looks exactly like my old dog, acts exactly like her and also seems to know me."

"Yeah thats pretty amazing. How long ago did you have the dog that looks like mine?"

Oh, several years ago, her name was Trixie and...."

The new dog jumped up at the sound of the name and starting wagging her tail.

"Thats amazing, she really seems to know you."

"Yeah, so where did you get her?"

"From an experimental station in New York."

"Long Island, New York?"

"Yes."

"Thats interesting, I visited a place out there where they sampled my old dog and took several DNA samples. They were considering cloning her because she had a great nose."

"This dog has the best nose I have ever seen, I think this is a product of your old dog's DNA."

"I wonder how many others they made."

"Oh quite a lot from what I saw, when I went to the kennels to select this dog there were at least 50 just like her."

"Wow, and the memory still seems to be there. What if they all remember me?"

"You should go there to find out, this is very weird."

"Weird or not, we need to get back to work, we're missing a lot of bags."

"Yep."

~~~~~~~~~~~~~~~~~~~~~~~~~~~~~~~

A few years later, a woman who had lost her husband in a plane crash had a similar experience. He had worked as an aerospace engineer and in similar fashion to the Trixie episode, had given some DNA to an experimental center in hopes to replicate his phenomenal mathematics talents. Years had passed after the accident and as the woman was drinking a latte at a local coffee store, she had that same "deja' vu" moment with a man she saw from a distance in the same store. He picked up his drink and turning around, saw her and dropped his cup on the floor.

"Josephine!" he yelled.

"Stephen?!"

"Yes it's me, where have you been?"

"Where have I been? What is going on here?"

The woman was stunned at one moment and upset at another. She put her hands to her mouth and stared as this perfect replication of her dead husband sat in front of her and seemed to know everything about her. They talked for a long time and both discovered that he had been confused about several things. No doubt he knew her in detail, it was just that the history around the time she had lost her husband was blurred.

"What are you doing here,?" she asked.

"Working locally on a rocket project."

"That's what my husband used to do."

"Interesting...did he work with antennas?"

"Yes, and he was the only one who understood the particular details of using them in space."

"As do I. In fact there are almost no antennas engineers in the U.S. now. They have all been replaced by young engineers who run simulation software. To them it does not matter if they are designing bridges or antennas, the efforts are the same. However to really understand designing bridges or antennas, you need specific training and experience. The engineers now don't realize that people like me wrote the equations they use. These equations are only a solution for a particular style of design, there are many more, some much better. This practice has slowed us down quite a bit so people like myself are in great demand."

"I wonder if they cloned you from my husband. Those are the exact words he used to describe his job so many years ago, its uncanny."

"Well I don't think so, I have memories from my childhood, adolescence and adult life."

"Ok, how about this...you were born in New York City."

"Yes, thats true."

"Your mother was an actress and your father a professor."

"That's true too!"

"This is very weird, okay one more question....when did you meet Josephine?"

"Well, that is a strange story. We met in an airplane, she was my flight instructor and giving me lessons when, at about 10,000 feet in the air she touched my hand by mistake. I thought I might be having feelings for her but was surprised at how good her touch felt. We flew on for another hour without discussing this then landed. After we tied the plane down, she came over, looked at me for a long time and asked if I would like to get some coffee. I knew we would not be talking about airplanes and felt very attracted to her. We had coffee and soon fell in love."

"Did she spill the coffee and say "Rats?"

"Yes, yes she did...she is kind of scary."

"For both of us, believe me."

"You know, when I first saw you, I thought you were my wife that I had not seen for a very long time."

"I had the same feeling for a moment, but this cannot be true. How long has it been since you last saw your wife?"

"Several years, she died in an airplane crash."

"So did my husband, he was flying to Allentown, Pennsylvania in a Cessna and iced up during the descent."

"A Cessna 210R model?"

"Yes, exactly. Red on white with a radar."

"And he complained that the radar was not working properly?"

"Yes...yes...this is very strange. Our stories both check out. It's impossible to have the same details with so many stories."

"Did they ever find the body?"

"No, that was a bit strange as well, the wreckage was found but no body. They think he might have fallen out."

"People just don't fall out, he or in my case she was strapped in well and the wind resistance to the doors especially with ice covering the plane, is immense. My Josephine was also not found, I am wondering if one of us is a clone."

"Is that possible?"

"Oh, yes, I have read and work in places, although I cannot give you any details, where clones have been made of talented individuals to either allow them to continue their important work or fulfill a talent need. In my world you have computer monkeys and a sprinkling of engineers who know what they are doing. Its cheaper that way."

"But how can we find out if one of us, and I will bet it is you, is a clone?"

"By comparing DNA samples, do you have anything left from your husband?"

"Somewhere I am sure I have at least a stand of hair."

"I will look for something from my wife as well."

They looked at each other for a long moment, realizing what probably had happened and walked away from each other without words. They knew they would meet in the same place the next day.

When they did meet the next day, all was not the same. Both of their lives had been changed forever and this gave them a new glint as they approached each other on the street.

"Good morning."

"Yes and an interesting one at that."

"Indeed."

"What are we going to do?"

"Live our lives, of course. But in a way others will probably not understand."

"How so?"

"You and I will always know I am the same but not the same. I have great memories of being with you; including a few fights. But I missed you when I left. To me it's a miracle to see you again but I am not the same person I once was. I know that that is a play on words but reality is I have different molecules than the original. Not that I am different, just not the same if you know what I mean."

"I do but I am curious about something."

"What's that?"

"Are there more of you?"

"I don't know but considering the reason for my existence in the first place I would not be surprised if there are many of me. It's a rare skill I have."

"It;s going to be very strange for me if I meet more of you, especially if you look identical and with the same memories."

"There will be differences."

"How so?"

"Only I have these present memories and the others are in different places."

"True."

"Do you want to stay together, I mean visit and talk frequently?"

"I am not sure about that, I have given you up for dead so long ago and I have been in other relationships. It's a bit confusing for me and I will have to think about it."

"Understood."

They paused for a long while then moved to sit down in front of a restaurant in anticipation of getting something to eat. She was obviously consumed by the recent events and he was somewhere between relief (to see her) and anger (that he was less than real). This reality set up two different paths for the two of them. She would wander a bit then take her own path after moving completely across the country and as far away from the memories as possible.

He on the other hand had another mission in mind. This mission would take him back to his birthplace and to Cape Canaveral to view a rocket launch of several of his brethren.

First, however, he needed to know about his origins.

They parted company with their new lives in focus. Characteristically, she went one way and he another. They would never see each other again except when she watched the news several years hence.

He left town that day for the island of his origin. As usual, it was highly guarded and very difficult to get to so the first step was to establish residency in a local town. He chose Sag Harbor, which was not too close to arise suspicion. He could take the ferry to Shelter Island and thence to Groton Connecticut to get a chance to see the island. The last ferry was large, slow and went by the island. He took pictures on several crossings as well as explore the various images available from space. Due to the secret nature of the work done on that island, most of the pictures were manufactured and did not show the important details of the buildings on the island.

His next step was to fly over the island in a small plane to take some pictures. Finding a flight instructor at Hampton airport, they flew around the area several times doing various maneuvers. At some point he asked to take pictures of the island, this made the instructor a bit nervous at first.

"I don't think we can do that, they do some secret government work out here."

"I am sure it's alright and in fact I heard that it is actually another island, maybe that one," he pointed to his left.

"Maybe, well okay lets go over there, I'd like to see it too."

They flew closer, but he knew that there was protected airspace right over the island and chose to fly the perimeter instead while he took pictures.

143

"Cool, got some good ones, thanks for letting me fly over here."

"No problem, man."

They returned to a nice touchdown and he went home to download the pictures and continue his research. There were very few guards, probably quite a lot of security cameras and plenty of wooded areas. He could probably get closer through the trees.

After staring at pictures for a few days, he made up his mind how to get there. Being an experienced scuba diver, he would take a small rubber dinghy on a moonless night to within a hundred yards or so, anchor out and swim the rest of the way in under water. After he emerged he would make his way through the woods until he found a way in or at least learned a lot more about the place.

Gathering his equipment, he chose to execute his plan on a late Sunday evening, getting the dinghy into the water on the Northern Fork of Long Island around midnight and rowing over to the island (which would take a few hours) and anchoring out downwind, just in case they had dogs. His equipment included night vision goggles, several air tanks, a scanning radio and a camera.

He found an isolated cove to get the boat in and started the adventure. The water was almost smooth, the moon was not out and it was generally cloudy. As he rowed out, he could barely see the island in the darkness. He rowed for well over an hour before he found the spot he had marked on a GPS receiver as the ingress point for his dive. The anchor was thrown over into about 50 feet of water and made fast. Donning his mask, flippers and BCD (buoyancy compensation device), he quickly slid over the side into the water. His wetsuit kept him from getting too cold and using his underwater compass he started the long swim to the island's shoreline. Luckily the current was not strong and the effort was not too arduous. He emerged right on schedule and quietly made his way onto the beach. The tank, flippers and mask were hidden carefully.

Now it was about four AM and all was quiet. He carefully made his way to the side of a building not covered with cameras and lights. Slowly he moved along the wall to a corner and peeked around briefly to view any activity. Seeing none, he moved along the next wall until he saw an opening between buildings where two guards were patrolling, or so he thought. They were walking between two other buildings but did not seem to be armed. They talked as they went and their voices sounded both familiar and as if they were twins. Although he could see one stop after a sentence and the other start in reply, the voice was identical. The familiarity came from the sense that they sounded just like him.

He needed more light to get a better understanding of what was going on so he retreated into the woods, dug a hole and carefully covered it with twigs and leaves. Then he retreated into it and waited until sunrise. He hoped that the dinghy was far enough away from shore to not be noticeable.

Waiting a few hours, the sun came up and he emerged again to make his way back to the protected wall. This time he could hear many voices, again all sounding the same. Again, he peeked around a corner and notice quite a few more people but this time he was shocked to see that they were all the same person and just like him! They were all clones of the same engineer that he once was. For his purposes now, this was good news; he would not stand out. However he was also in a wet suit and that needed to be changed. Back into the woods he went and he circled the compound until he found the housing area. Then, looking for an open back door, he entered carefully, made sure no one was home and found clothes in a bedroom. He changed quickly, found a large plastic bag for his wetsuit, combed his hair and made his way out the same way he came in. Now he was much less conspicuous and could walk about freely.

Walking confidently, he made his way back to the area near the shore were he had emerged and stashed his wetsuit near his other gear. He made sure no one saw him, then stood up and walked back to the center of the compound to start his recon operation.

There were quite a few buildings made up of laboratories, housing units, cafeterias and offices. Most of the population was identical to him with a sprinkling of others, obviously the scientists and bioengineers who were in charge of this project. Everyone ignored him and after an hour of so of exploring the outside areas, he then decided to make his way into a laboratory to determine what the purpose of the clone colony really was.

Listening to conversations gave him clues to their purpose. The clones referred to themselves by numbers.

"Hello. Five."

"Hello. I am Six to get the phase one report."

"Here they are...good day."

"And to you as well."

He listened as much as possible then determined that few questions were asked, only tasks were accomplished here. He also determined that there could be at least 50 of the clones based on the numbers he overheard. There were gaps in the numbers, typically between counts of ten. For instance he did not hear anyone with names 11 to 20. He assumed they were elsewhere. He also noticed that the speech was monotone, as if they were programmed and without emotion. They moved about without changing their gaze from straight ahead. If he followed this protocol, he could become invisible and travel about at will.

Inside the laboratory he found several researchers looking through microscopes and probing petri dishes. One looked up at him and seemed to expect a response. He made it simple.

"Nine."

"Please take these samples to building four, lab twenty one."

He took the Nalgene box and left the lab, thankful for having passed the first test.

Now he had to find building four. He walked outside passing several other people and observing that the building had numbers on the upper left side as viewed from the central common area, made his way to the appropriate building. This particular building was much more advanced than the first one he was in. It contained very sophisticated labs with large computer systems, cryogenic freezers, operating rooms and quite a few more "non him" people. The labs were numbered based on the floor they were on. As he was looking for lab twenty one, he went upstairs and discovered the sequential numbering of the labs, walked to the correct one and entered.

One of the scientists looked up and waited for a response.

"Nine."

Reaching out to take the sample, the scientist said "thank you."

He was not sure as to what to do next so he paused then started to leave.

"Stay here, nine."

Without speaking he moved back to the same spot he had occupied when he handed over the package.

"That was weird," said another scientist. "I have not seen one of this type go autonomous."

The first scientist replied, "probably a lab four experiment. They are trying to get these units to think for themselves."

"Hope they don't make a mistake again like the one that escaped, he had no idea he was manufactured."

147

"Did they every find him?"

"They think he might be in Miami."

"Hope they get him, it could be very embarrassing if they don't."

"Indeed."

He stood there silently, listening to the comments and keeping his eyes focused straight ahead. The scientists and engineers finally lost interest and concentrated on their work. However, they did chatter back and forth about the details of their endeavors.

"I am getting close on this mood modifier enzyme," said one scientist.

"I heard, congratulations. You have worked very hard on it. Is it stable?"

"Pretty much, it's passing all of the tests now. However I just want to make sure and see how it reacts in non-orthodox situations."

"Good. We can't have it go haywire."

"Nope. This one's important and programs the emotion centers of the brain to remain calm and follow instructions no matter what is going on around it."

"Perfect for spaceflight, huh?"

"As is all of our work," he said smiling back.

He continued to stand still but his mind was racing. "What are they talking about? What is this business about spaceflight?"

The first scientist continued, "These drones will encounter a lot of challenges on their way to the stars, but at least we can trust what they will do once they find a place for us."

"Yes, and their programming is so complete they will be able to withstand the rigor of space travel including the harsh radiation."

"I worked on that task last year. You can almost burn these things up without any problems with their routines. They just keep on ticking!"

"They take a licking and keep on ticking!"

"Ha! Very funny."

Looking at him, the first scientist said, "Take these samples to lab 16, building four."

He took the plastic box and exited. One of the scientist followed him out with his eyes.

"That one is a bit different."

"A bit. Probably an "A" model."

"Yeah, probably."

He walked out and started towards building four. He intended to go in but exit through another door. He needed to find out more about the space flight aspect the scientists were referring to. What did it mean? If drones were going to space for a long distance stellar flight, were humans going as well? He guessed that they would not be going along based on their sensitivity to space radiation. What he had to do now was go back home and research any details about the space voyages on the Internet. Then if necessary plan a return visit. He had been lucky, very lucky to not get stopped.

Just so it would not be obvious that he was an imposter, he went to lab 16. Luckily it was not occupied so he left the plastic container on a lab bench and exited. Finding a rear door, he left smartly and found his way back into the forest. Carefully, he returned to his stashed his wet suit and diving gear, donned it, hid the normal clothes in the plastic bag he had used before and buried it in a dry place in case he needed them again.

It was late in the day and this side of the island was on the East side and thus darker now than the other side. Walking backwards into the water, he scanned for any activity and lowered himself quickly into the cove. He held held his breath, turned around towards the waiting dinghy and kept from breathing until he ran out of air, so the bubbles from his scuba regulator would not be detected. After a 20 minute underwater swim he found the anchor line and slowly came up and crawled in. The anchor was raised and he started his rowing away from the island and back to where his truck was waiting.

By the time he got there it was fully dark so getting his equipment out and stowed in the truck drew no attention. Changing into dry clothes, he drove back home to Sag Harbor to consider his experience.

Once safely at home, he wrote down notes about the experience and tried to remember everything he had heard. Then he started to research anything about drone production and space travel. He looked at the professional journals and started to find bits and pieces of the story as many of the scientists had published results of their accomplishments. The idea of programming the brains of drones was written between the lines in several papers. It was not talked about explicitly because the activity was classified. There was simply the implication that it was highly possible. Other papers discussed modification technologies and the range of control they could have on the drones. It became clear after reading many papers that there was a path from drone production to the total programming of their minds.

He was stunned as he read more and considered his experience. It sounded like they were producing drones to take the place of human astronauts for long duration space flight. They could fill their brains with all of the necessary information on conducting the flight. They could also fill their brains with activities necessary to prepare a foreign world for human habitation. Then what? What would happen to the drones, would they simply morph into automaton mode? Would they turn into slaves?

He had to know more-these drones would represent our society when they landed on another planet. What would the inhabitants think? Scary thought.

It became extremely important for him to get as much information as possible on this mission including whether or not he had been modified (his body anyway) to withstand such a long flight.

He spend hour upon hour searching the Internet for clues and details. Again, he watched all of the professional journals and after a week of intensive study came up with the following details:

Ten drones will be sent on a large rocket currently being built secretly at Cape Canaveral.

They will be put in hibernation for a flight to Gliese 581g, otherwise known as Zarmina. This will take years, at least 20 depending on the speed of the spacecraft.

The rocket will take the drones to an orbiting space station and after docking, will make the journey together.

The only reasonable way to get humans to space is to "radiation harden" them, initially using drones as they are considered expendable.

This knowledge filled him with both anger and concern. The drones would not represent human beings well at all, especially as scientists and people with emotions, curiosity and the like. It was important for him to consider the options and make the right decision. Should he expose this program to the general public? If so, it would be canceled and the quest to visit the stars would be delayed by many years, maybe permanently if the space radiation issue cannot be solved for human flight. Should he try to intervene? How could he do this, and for what purpose?

He considered the second option, intervening as the best hope to have proper representation on the space voyage. He felt very compelled (programmed?) to participate and also felt like he knew more details about the program than he had learned from reading in the journals. It was a sub-conscious type of understanding where he felt that his intuition was guiding him more than his observable senses. He took the next steps and decided to move to Florida, integrate himself into the astronaut corp and find a way to travel to Zarmina. Although this was both ambitious and dangerous, somehow he knew it was an achievable goal and thus, worth pursuing with all of his heart and soul.

He packed his bags, cleaned up any evidence that he had been on Long Island, and drove to Cocoa Beach, Florida. His excitement allowed him to drive the distance in one very long day, arriving at a Starbuck's coffee store right before it closed one evening. He was tired and hungry and decided to use the drive-thru instead of going in. A well groomed barista named Stephen was at the window and with a bit of personal panache, gave him a well made drink and a sandwich.

"Thank you."

"Of course, Sir, have a nice evening."

He drove down the main street and looked for a reasonable hotel to stop at. Finding one, he went in with his drink and food, signed the appropriate paperwork and made his way to his room.

Exhausted and energized at the same time, he ate, drank and watched a bit of TV. While he was sitting there strung out from the road he considered his place in nature.

Am I real? Do I have the same rights as any other human being? For now, people on the outside think I am real and people on the "inside" know I am not. That's going to be a hard transition to make. But I have to make it, there needs to be representation on this voyage, we can't just send automatons out into the Universe.

He thought about these issues for a bit longer, then his mind went blank with sleep.

Waking up many hours later, he found himself still in his clothes with food on the floor covered in ants and a spilled coffee drink.

"Swell."

A shower and shave was next, helping to clear the cobwebs. He ate breakfast downstairs. It had been a long drive and the effects were still pronounced. He decided to have a relaxed day as he felt somehow that the launch would not be for a few months. After breakfast, he cleaned out his car and drove to Jetty Park, just south of the rocket launch towers in Port Canaveral. He drove in after paying the attendant, found an open area on the large canal and backed his car in. He pulled out a lawn chair and a hat from the trunk, sat down and started to watch the traffic going in and out of the port. It was by now a bit late in the afternoon and other cars were filing in and parking. He wondered why but soon overheard an explanation.

"They start at about 4:30."

"Is Carnaval first or Disney?"

"Usually Carnaval."

He realized they were talking about cruise ships as he had noticed several of them tied up on his way into the park. Now however the ones he could see from his chair were running, as could be seen by the faint smoke coming out of their smokestacks.

Right around 4:30, as predicted, one of the giant cruise ships started to move away from its dock. It made its way to the center of the canal and towards the sea. It was huge, spectacular and filled with partygoers who were hanging on the rails waving at the people in the park.

He waved instinctively.

Within ten minutes another cruise ship went by, this time it was the Disney ship, full of families with kids and groups of partiers waving to the people at the park. They played 'Wish upon a Star' with the ship's air horns as it went by. He smiled at the sound and thought about all of those people having a great time for the next several days. They would eat well and stop in the Bahamas to shop, but mostly the ship was the attraction with a mall, theaters, fun classes for kids and bars for the adults. It looked like a good time for all.

"Nice ship, huh?"

He looked up to see a blonde woman standing about six feet away with her hand shielding her eyes from the fun and looking at the ship.

"Beautiful, I'll bet they are going to have a great time."

"I prefer the small ships, the ones that go into the Aegean or the Galapagos."

"That would be a blast, an experience of a lifetime."

"Yes indeed. So...is this your first time viewing the parade of ships?"

"Yep, first time. It very nice out here, peaceful with lots of things to see on the water."

"Yeah, I love it. This will sound strange, but I come out here where all of these people are to relax and get away from things."

"You don't realize they are here when you are looking at the water though."

"True, you can't hear them either."

"So you come out here often?"

"I do, mind if I sit down?"

"Of course not, that would be great."

"Yeah, I come out here pretty often, sometimes to see the ships and sometimes not. As soon as these ships all pass by the crowd will disappear. It gets real peaceful then."

"Sounds idyllic."

"Oh it is, it allows me to contemplate the world around us and what it means."

"Oooo, a philosopher!"

"Yes by training, I teach at a local college."

"What type of philosophy do you teach?"

"Logic, epistemology, phenomenology, existentialism and the classics."

"Good group."

"Yes, in fact; pretty much covers the highlights of philosophic thought."

"And you find yourself here watching boats and crazy people hanging over the rails."

"Ha! Yeah I guess that looks a little suspicious. Actually I come out here to watch humanity sail by in a happy mood, then enjoy the peace that follows. The animals seem to return, the locals go back to their beer and I sit here watching the slow movement of the water."

"And an occasional rocket launch."

"Oh yes, and those are spectacular from this close," she pointed North to the land just on the other side of the canal. "They leave the Earth from over there, with bright light and a roar to follow. I think about how all of this activity is just a prelude to humans traveling to the stars. I wrote my dissertation on what we will become out there."

"Thats a serious question I have been asking myself lately."

"Indeed? So what brings you to the park today?"

"Well, lots of things really. But most of all to understand what we are launching and why. I am an engineer in fact, an antenna designer and have had the privilege to work on quite a few spacecraft systems. Now I am interested in the overall consequences of our quest for the stars, I am thinking about writing a book about it."

"And a good book that would be. We are moving to the stars as if by some unseen force. We are pulled in that direction, much like the explorers who moved West into the wilderness during the 17 and 1800s. They call it the last frontier, which

I think is partially true. There is a famous saying, 'No matter where you go, there you are' attributed to Confucius. We will spend a lot of time and energy to find ourselves out there. It's worth the effort, don't get me wrong but our brains are getting stronger and with the integration of technology as it is happening now, we will move faster in our quest to understand everything."

"Yes, I am familiar with that type of technology."

"How so?"

"Oh, I read a lot."

"And what do you think about our future out there in the stars?"

"An amazingly important question because I wonder what we will be when we get there, those aliens will meet who? People like you and I? Or people that have been selected, conditioned and optimized?"

She looked at him for an extended period and then choose her words carefully.

"They are doing something soon here that I am concerned about relative to your last comment."

"Do you have any details about this?"

"Well, a friend of mine works at the Cape and although he has a Top Secret clearance, has led me to believe that something special or weird, depending on how you look at it, is happening within a few months. It has to do with a large rocket and an attempt to go to Zarmina."

"Zarmina?"

"Yes, it's a planet much like Earth that was discovered a while ago. It has about the same temperature and gravity; although it is tidal locked it has a nice temperate zone which could harbor life."

"How far away is it?"

"About 20 light years, which is a very long time to be staring out of the window, so they will have to figure out something, I just don't know the details."

"Hmmm They will either have to find a way to hibernate or make the ship so big that they live their normal lives for a generation or so."

"Or send special humans," she said this as she averted her eyes.

"What do you mean by special?"

"Modified, I think. I really don't know, its just rumor. My friend really can't talk about it but others tell me that they can do something with humans so they are like robots and won't go crazy on such a long trip."

"Wow. Thats amazing," he said looking across the canal at the Cape installation.

"Yes, but I think that is a real problem."

"How so?"

"They are not sending 'Us' out there, just partial 'Us.'

"Yes I completely understand, there is really danger by doing that, on a lot of fronts."

"I hope the rumors are not true, this really concerns me."

"Me too."

They sat there in silence for quite a while. One contemplating a rumor, the other a reality. Finally, at some point he realized that he wanted to know her name.

"This has been nice talking to you, what's your name?"

"Savanna."

"And yours?"

"I think it's Stephen."

"You think?"

"Yeah, its a long story, but I am a drone that was created from the DNA of an engineer named Stephen. I will be part of the crew that goes to Zarmina."

"Ok, this conversation just got weird quickly," she said looking suspiciously at him.

"Sorry," he said smiling wryly, "it really is Stephen and I thought it would be interesting to see if you had a problem with drones."

"Whew, I really thought you were saying you were a drone, which would have scared me. I mean, I don't have anything against the idea except that it causes a great moral dilemma that will have to be dealt with someday."

"What's that?"

"Are they fully human beings? Or are they replicas?"

"I am not sure myself. Over the last 100 years we have modified ourselves to be better; first through vaccinations, then bionic parts, then genetic enhancements and now they make drones of dogs and sheep."

"Yes I know and I would guess human drones are not far behind. In a strange way it would make sense to send them to the stars. They are expendable aren't they?"

"I don't think a drone would think so. They are fully conscious and believe they are completely human albeit a copy."

"You know, you are scaring me again."

"Sorry, I have been doing a lot of reading about this subject lately. It's just seeping into my brain."

"Oh, okay."

"So...as a philosopher, how would you feel if we were visited by aliens from 20 light years away that were facsimiles of their real species?"

"It would depend if I knew the truth or not."

"So if they did not tell you, then you would assume that their culture was as they presented it?"

"I suppose, but that's a great question. The only information we could use would be their behavior and the story they told. Actually, it could get very interesting if they were the clones of the same person, assuming they all came together to explore our world. So if they were all the same person we could assume that their whole species was the same as well, unless told otherwise. But on the other hand, if the clone was alone we might not know, even if we did extensive biological testing."

"But again, as a philosopher, it would be their reality, and just as legitimate as ours wouldn't it?"

"I suppose so, it's an easy question if they are the ones who define reality."

"Yes, I hope so."

"There you go again, Stephen, scaring me. Let's take it from a different angle. What will you be doing for the next few days?"

"Exploring this area, visiting the Space center, and a few other things."

"Okay, good, sounds like legitimate activities. I might have to make a phone call if you told me you were going to join your clone buddies and head out to, what did you call it, Zarima?"

"Zarmina. And we have space for you if your interested."

"Very funny but no thanks, I choose to stay grounded."

"You *are* a philosopher! Is staying grounded where all of the answers are?"

"All of the answers are going to pass through your mind, whether in the past, now or in the future. That's all you will be given, so it's best to read, ask questions, explore, then make a conclusion. So I will let you fly boys go out into the heavens and send me more mental food."

"Okay, shall do, Plato."

"Well, thank you for the stimulating conversation, I need to go home and prepare a new lecture on clone consciousness for tomorrow's class."

"Yes, I appreciated our talk. And yes, keep your eyes, ears and mind open with regards to the activities around here. It could be interesting."

She got up, folded her chair and packed it into the trunk of her car. As she moved to the driver's door, she waved.

He smiled back and thought about the tricky conversation they just had. It was important not to get too serious about the drone story however he was desperate to know what other's would (will) think once it does get out into the public. For now, however he just sat back and relaxed. He stayed until just after dusk, watching the fishing boats and the twinkling lights of the launch platforms in the distance.

Then he packed up and went back to his hotel to plan his next move. What he had decided was to somehow use his clone self to get into the flight preparation area of the space center, just like he did back in New York. He studied the maps of the launch facility and read as much as he could over the next few days. He also tested himself by drawing the building layout and while pointing at the squares and rectangles, called out the name or number and what he thought could be going on in there.

After he felt he was ready, he again used his scuba skills and quietly entered the facility on the ocean side very late one evening. He used the cover of the indigenous vegetation to keep hidden while he examined how people were dressed and their general activities. He noticed very casual attire on several of the clones. He would not be noticed if he casually walked around. After a few more minutes he decided to do just that. He stood up, brushed off his clothes, got his mind 'in character' and walked out onto the sidewalk that went between two buildings. As he did so, he noticed that the setting of scientists and engineers was roughly the same as he had witnessed before in Long Island. He also noticed the affect of the clones, serious and with purpose as they moved about from building to building.

After about 20 minutes of walking around and getting a sense of the layout and purpose of the facility, he walked into the door of the biggest laboratory. It was much cooler in there than the Florida heat and felt very comfortable. As he walked down the hallways, he listened to conversations and observed the general activity and purpose. It looked like this particular lab was used for mission simulations and he saw several clones suited up. He did not see anyone other than clones suited up and came to the conclusion that his intuition about the mission was pretty accurate. In fact, while he was now in the main activity area, much of the mission was becoming very clear. He felt like he knew about the main propulsion, navigation and communication systems. Again, it was like intuition but he felt like he had been programmed to be familiar with many aspects of this mission. This knowledge would make it much easier to blend in.

For the rest of the day, he walked around from lab to lab. At one point during his explorations, he went into a communications and radar systems lab and found himself very familiar and comfortable. He interacted briefly with the others, who seemed to totally accept his presence. By the end of the day, his brain was full and he felt like he had to make his escape. The sun had gone down and as he walked to the Eastern end of the compound, it was easy for him to slip into the shadows and make his way back to his scuba gear. He found it where he had buried it and changed into his wetsuit and put on his BCD and air tank. Carefully he walked into the water, crouching down to be less conspicuous. Once out into about four feet of water, he dove down slowly and made his way to the offshore dinghy. He rowed back to his secluded beach and came out in darkness. His truck was waiting where he had left it. He packed it and after covering the bed, drove home to the hotel. That night after dinner he thought about his experiences and decided to completely integrate himself into the facility the next day. There was only one problem: at some point, the people there would notice that there was one extra clone training for the mission. He had to think his way around this.

The best approach would be to identify one of the clones who would have similar skills as he did, then send the clone on a long mission somewhere while he took his place. This would require both he and the clone to be in the same proximity for a while. This would be tricky.

The next day he finalized his plan and that evening he again took his dinghy out and anchored in a secluded cove to keep from getting attention. Early the next morning, he again walked confidently amongst the others, noticing their badges and keeping track of who went where. Again, he found himself in laboratories or high bay areas with simulators. Again, his subconscious spoke to him, which he had learned to listen to, and guided him to a communications lab with only a single drone working on it. After looking through the window, he walked in and started a conversation with the drone. No one else was in the lab at that time.

"Hello 12."

"Hello, can I help you?"

"Yes, I am from the central lab, where we are both originally from, they have a special mission for you that must be completed before our launch date."

"Please describe it."

"The senior scientists are concerned that none of us has any survival skills on the ocean, you must obtain the necessary experience in case we have a problem during our launch or landing at Zarmina."

"I understand."

"You will brief me on your work here then I will take you to a marina to teach you how to sail. You will then take a voyage and return."

"I understand."

"First I need to have you get a copy of your badge, you must give me yours and go to the security office and tell them that you have lost your badge. You may not tell them of my visit as this will upset the senior scientists. We are under strict orders to follow their instructions."

"I understand, here is my badge."

The clone then stood up and made his way to the security office to obtain another badge. Stephen stayed in the lab reading notebooks, and getting to know the nature of the work being performed in the lab.

Soon the clone returned and proceeded to describe his work in detail. Stephen followed effortlessly as this was what he had been programmed to do.

At the end of the work shift, Stephen instructed the clone to meet him at the Ocean club marina in Port Canaveral at seven that evening. They met up in the parking lot and walked down the docks in search of a sail boat for sale. After the third dock they found a 49 foot Hunter. It looked like it was in excellent shape; he noted the phone number and after a good long look, they walked back to their cars.

"Ok I will purchase that boat and see you at the lab tomorrow morning. And remember you cannot tell anyone about this mission as it will upset the senior scientists."

"Understood."

They left to their respective homes, number twelve to the barracks on the compound and he to the hotel room.

That night he called the number and negotiated a fair price. The seller was pleased that Stephen did not insist on a survey, haul out or sea trial.

The next few days, Stephen worked on the financing of the boat and spent most of his time in the lab with number 12. The clone was more like an automaton, with no emotions, will or ambition. He had been designed to serve. Stephen learned how to best manipulate his personality and also learned about the details of his place on the ship. He was to be the communications and radar officer. Both a perfect match for their training and original source of life.

Stephen took ownership of the boat Friday of that week. He promptly moved in and started to review all of its systems and to make sure it was seaworthy and capable of a long voyage. After a day on board he felt like he had made a good choice, the boat had been kept in perfect condition including a detailed sailing log and documentation on the engines and electronics. It had been to Bermuda, the Bahamas and to the Virgin Islands over the last few years and had been outfitted properly for long voyages.

On the following Monday, he instructed number 12 to meet him at the sailboat that evening, which he did. They discussed navigation and weather that night. The next night they met again and discussed the systems on board the vessel. It was easy to teach number 12 as he had perfect recall of all details once taught. The next day, they raised and lowered the sails and discussed when to use what sails when out at sea. The following day they took the boat out into the Atlantic, first by inboard engine power then, as they cleared the canal, by sail. They practiced tacking and went over emergency procedures. They also went over the operation of the onboard Ham radio, which number 12 was to use everyday reporting his position and listening for further instructions.

The last several days, Stephen observed while number 12 sailed the boat in varying conditions. He always kept a harness on and had easy access to a life preserver. They agreed on a special code that only they understood that would be used to report his position every night at 9:00 local time, wherever that may be. The real time the message was received would also tell approximately where the boat was in Longitude. Number 12 would use his GPS to report his detailed position and then back the numbers up with a sextant and chronometer.

Within a full week, Stephen realized that number 12 was good to go. He had absorbed as much knowledge from the lab as possible, number 12 was experienced enough to be safe for his first few legs of sailing and they had a communications link that would allow Stephen to assist number 12 in the event of a problem.

The next day they filled the boat with food and water.

"Okay, you are ready to go. The senior scientists said that you to go to the Bahamas first, then down the island chain to Panama. You are to go through the locks and sail up the coast until you get to the Baja de California, then you will sail directly to Tahiti. I will contact you periodically with new instructions. You will not discuss the details of the journey with anyone, as we talked about several times. Do you understand?"

"I understand. When do I depart?"

"Now."

With that, number 12 mechanically prepared the sailboat for an ocean journey, tying down everything that could come loose if he encountered bad weather. He did not talk as Stephen stood on the dock watching. When his tasks were complete, he cast off and used the internal engine to make his way into the canal and out to sea. Stephen watched until he disappeared then went back to his truck to monitor the Ham radio. Within an hour it was 9:00 pm and number 12 reported his position in the agreed code format, then waited for a response which Stephen gave, then kept on sailing.

Stephen found an apartment near the Cape that was on a top floor of a tall building, he strung a wire antenna out of the window and every night monitored the radio for the position report. The scientists at the cape did not have a problem with him moving out of the barracks as he had long ago spent time on the sailboat and had not reported his latest move. Number 12 was making good progress and keeping safe but did not realize that he would be out to sea for over a month, well beyond the launch date of the interstellar spaceship.

Meanwhile Stephen worked in the lab, spent time in the simulators, kept a flat affect and prepared for a trip into space.

That day came soon enough, he packed his belongings and brought them into his "old" room at the Cape, then that evening made contact with number 12 who was on his way across the Pacific Ocean; he instructed him to return and live at the barracks again.

Then the entire team of drones reported to the launch facility, got suited up and took their places in the spaceship. The first part was to make orbit, then mate up with a larger ship that had been build robotically in space. The complete assembly was then to rocket to Zarmina over the next 30 years. There were 9 drones and Stephen, who would place themselves in hibernation until a few weeks away from entering orbit. Then they would come alive, report any interesting details and after de-mating the smaller spaceship from the assembly, land on the surface of the planet.

They arrived as planned, Stephen immediately looked at the communication logs and found that number 12 had in fact returned safely, moved into the barracks and it was assumed that he was the lone drone who had escaped so many months ago. They reprogrammed him and set him to other tasks. The incident was then forgotten.

Meanwhile, Stephen looked at the other drones performing their tasks mechanically and realized he was the only human aboard.

GRACE AND STARDEN

"My disability exists not because I use a wheelchair, but because the broader environment isn't accessible" - *Stella Young*

Post death, dark until they get the camera working, etc. Mechanical love prevails, how is it manifested?

Grace and Starden spent a lot of time together. They lived together, played together and when they had nothing in particular to do, they sat together. They were like opposite magnetic poles of equal magnitude; they were drawn together by equal forces. It wasn't demanded or coerced or created by

167

strange psychological forces, it was just a natural way to live. Neither one of them had had any previous experiences like this so it wasn't learned behavior it, as stated before, but truly natural.

So it came to pass that, and again they were together for this, an opportunity to fly in a small plane and view their city from the sky. It was a beautiful day with very light winds and when they became airborne, it was glass smooth. The pilot, a friend of theirs, had just received his private pilot's license and was eager to get more experience by taking his friends and family for fun flights. These are flights that have little or no risk, where the weather has to be perfect, there are no long cross countries, they stay close to home and no aerobatics. Just plain fun.

They climbed through the clean morning air on their way to 2,000 feet above the ground to fly over to their neighborhood and other sites. Grace and Starden sat together in the back of the four place high wing aircraft, looking out the windows and taking pictures. The pilot was expecting one of them to sit up front and maybe get a chance to hold the controls briefly, but the couple seemed uninterested in either flying or sitting apart.

They leveled off and the pilot adjusted some controls to lower the engine's rpms. The sound level went down quite a bit, the engine noise was partially replaced with wind noise as they started to accelerate. The pilot banked the plane and tried to control it smoothly to give the effect of a much larger airliner in flight. He did a decent job in this deception.

The couple was lost in their observations and the general thrill of flying like a bird above the houses, traffic and heat. The pilot however was checking gauges as he should and was getting a bit concerned about indications that he had not experienced before. The RPM gauge was fluctuating a bit and the Exhaust Gas Temperature (or EGT for short) was climbing. Other gauges were showing nominal behavior but something just did not feel right. He chose to keep cool, monitor everything and keep flying.

Then the engine quit. The pilot, being a bit inexperienced, did not fly the plane first, he tried instead to diagnose the problem. He played with the mixture and throttle controls then looked at the circuit breakers. What he should have done was "aviate, navigate and communicate," a mantra drilled into all pilots. By not aviating or flying the plane he let his altitude drop too far and thus gave away range for a safe off-airport landing. The plane was not at best glide speed either nor was he looking around for a suitable place to land. He kept fooling around in the cockpit. The passengers were getting concerned as a wing dipped or he would abruptly pull the nose up. As a result of his lack of focus on the basics of flying, all too soon he had to make a very quick decision on where to land due to the fact that the ground was coming up very rapidly. Within seconds he had to choose landing on a house or go into a forest of trees. Still not aviating he let the speed decay until the left wing stalled and then dipped, giving him no control on the flight path of the aircraft. The plane fell 100 feet into a group of trees, the nose rotated down and they hit the ground very hard. The pilot was knocked out and fuel was leaking, he had also forgotten to turn the electrical power off and close all of the fuel valves. Fire was imminent. Grace and Starden were badly bruised and had been crushed between the forward seats and the back of the plane. Starden had the insight to punch out one of the side windows and reeling from a broken back, managed to make his way out of the plane, immediately turning to pull Grace out with him. She also had a broken back and was in great pain. He pulled both of them as far away as possible from the wreckage when it exploded in flames. Several aluminum projectiles hit them as well as an intense heat wave. He continued to pull them away until they made it to the lawn of a house where he collapsed. The occupants of the house were outside now and called the emergency services and were trying to tend to the two crumpled people on their lawn. Both were breathing but not responding to questions.

The police, fire department and ambulances showed up within minutes and after a triage, stabilized Grace and Starden then got them on stretchers to transport them to a close hospital. There both had oxygen cannulas in their noses and had IVs started to decrease their blood loss. Within minutes they were being wheeled into the emergency room. The pilot had not made it out of the wreckage and was pronounced dead at the scene of the crash.

Both Grace and Starden spent the next few hours undergoing surgery to fix collapsed lungs, ribcages and broken bones. Both had crushed vertebrae and spinal columns. After surgery they were sent to the intensive care unit to start the healing process. They spent many days there until they were able to talk and understand what had happened. They also asked immediately about the status of the other and then asked the beds to be put in the same room. Initially the hospital staff denied their request but after much complaining from the pair and senior doctor told the staff to find a way to comply with their wishes. He understood they would heal faster together instead of apart.

Soon they were told the extent of their injuries and the prognosis for a full recovery. The doctors and a few nurses gathered in their room one day and gave them the following news:

"You both are mending as well as could be expected but due to the seriousness of your injuries we are looking at a long hard road ahead. I am not going to sugar coat this or give you any false hopes, but the reality is that you both have severe spinal cord injuries and will be confined to a wheelchair for rest of your lives. I'm sorry, we worked extremely hard on you and made sure you had every chance to achieve full recovery but you both experienced massive spinal cord injuries and severe trauma to your lower extremities. We have been testing for any signs of nerve recovery every day since you were brought into ICU but the reality is that there was just too much damage. Now, that being said, you still will be able to live a good long life and there are many support groups and physical therapy options for you to choose from. Over the several days we will be moving you out of the beds and into chairs. Your insurance will pay for electric mobility devices that will allow you to live a near normal life. Do you have any questions?"

"Near normal?"

"Yes, you will not be able to walk or support your own weight with your legs, you will have limited use of your arms but with training and hard work we think you can learn how to get around. There are lots of programs to choose from that specialize in your types of injuries. The best medicine by far is to keep a positive attitude."

"We understand. Did we have an cranial injuries or reason to worry about our mental capabilities?"

"No, none. Mentally you are in good shape, however you should consider counseling as part or your healing process."

Starden looked at Grace.

"At least we still have each other."

She smiled even though it probably hurt her to do so.

The doctors asked for further questions but they had none. Now it was time to deal with the aftermath and find a way to exist with the limitations.

Within a week, they were transferred to a physical therapy wing of the hospital and then, with new battery powered wheelchairs, allowed to go home. Their friends picked them up and moved them and their new contraptions back home. Grace and Starden were amazed at how difficult it was to get around when bound to a chair. Every detail of their lives was affected by this. However at the end of these frustrating days they still managed to find time to sit together and watch TV, typically while holding hands.

A few months went by and being intelligent people, they found new activities on the Internet, including research. The learned as much as possible about their injuries, micro-neural surgery techniques and the chances of improving their situation. Very little hope was found given the extent of their injuries but as time went by they were able to get better control of their arms although absolutely nothing from their legs. Nurses visited daily to make sure they were okay. Most of the nurses had a not-so-well concealed look of pity on them. This made Grace and Starden uncomfortable as they could only look forward now and not feel bad about their new lives. At some point a new nurse came in, fresh from the Army and battlefield experienced. He did not have any pity and after they got to know him, he told them that he did not understand why they were not doing more for themselves.

"You're in a rut."

"Why to you say that?"

"Well, I have been coming here for a few months now, your guys seemed settled into a routine, reasonably happy, doing all you can in terms of physical therapy but for some reason you have given up on your research regarding your condition."

"That's because there is nothing more to learn about it."

"That will never be true."

"How can you say that? We have spent a thousand hours researching our condition. Its hopeless."

"That's bullshit."

"Easy for you to say."

"No it isn't, I am risking alienating you, which I don't want to do. I have other patients who are in worse shape and have never given up, yet others who are in better shape and who have given up. It's all psychological. You don't understand that there are mediocre minds with PhDs and geniuses who sweep the streets. It's just a matter of doing the work. You two have wonderful minds and it would be a real shame if you gave up and wasted your capabilities."

"We appreciate your concern but this is who we are now. We will be okay, especially if we are together."

The nurse shook his head and went back to his duties, mumbling to himself periodically. Starden looked at Grace for a bit as she looked back silently.

"That guy is a pain in the ass."

"Except he is right, we have slipped into mediocrity, far from what we used to be."

"Yeah, well there is not much more we can do now, is there?"

"I don't know, there has to be something, even if we have to be creative."

"I'm too tired to be creative."

"I'm tired too but if anyone can figure out something interesting, it is us. Now come on, quite whining."

"Oh all right, I will start thinking about this....tomorrow."

He smiled at her when he said this, she frowned.

"No later than tomorrow!"

The next day he was up earlier than usual and working the Internet. He also started thinking 'old school' and decided to go to the local University's library and talk to actual people. She went on-line and decided not to research their malady on purpose but to take a completely new approach and research mobility. They spent an unusual amount of time apart as he was gone for most of the day and she was transfixed on the computer screen. They met later that night for dinner.

"Did you get anywhere?"

"I think so, but I have a long way to go."

"Well, I am glad we are making the effort. I found some ideas on the Internet.

173

"Yeah, and I talked to several people at the University. It was interesting, they had no pity just curiosity."

"Curiosity about what?"

"Well maybe it's my imagination but they had a sense of wonderment or maybe respect that I was in a chair. I have not experienced that before."

"Where did you go?"

"To the electrical engineering department."

"Why there?"

"They are great problem solvers."

"Did they say anything interesting?"

"Yes."

"What?"

"They think we should be robots."

"Yeah, right. That's funny. You can be R2 and I will be CP3O."

"Kinda," he said with a straight face.

"Alright, what do you mean?"

"They have a large robotics focus at the department. This includes machine learning and mechanical systems. It seems they have some of the best researchers in the field there. They brought me into a conference room, gave me coffee and in came about 20 professors and grad students. First they showed me a power point presentation on their creations, including autonomous robots, self-driving cars, UAVs, autopilots for jet aircraft, and finally, working with paraplegics."

"Yes, and?"

"The work was initially started at the Jet Propulsion Laboratories in Pasadena, California, right next to Caltech. They implanted electrodes in the legs of paraplegics, programmed a computer to activate the electrodes in certain canned sequences, gave the person a small joystick placed on his index finger and then trained him to walk, go up stairs, go down stairs, sit, etc. The person had to have a belt-worn computer and battery pack. The system worked for about 10 minutes between charges. That was in the 1990s. Now they have advanced significantly and have been looking for people like us for a long time, especially us."

"Sounds interesting. Why do you say they have been looking for people like us?"

"Because we can help each other during the transition."

"Transition to what?"

"Robots."

"Okay, I'm sorry that does not make any sense to me."

"Well, here's the deal: they want people like us to have prosthetic arms and legs built around us and essentially the rest of our bodies encased in a protective shell. They have a lot of money from DARPA to support their work."

"So we would become the central nervous system to a machine?"

"In a way, yes."

"Hmmm, I have to think about this. What are the advantages?"

"The advantages are that we would be fully mobile and do any physical activity we used to do, including screwing."

"Well, okay, I see where your priorities are. What about the disadvantages?"

"We have to charge up periodically, probably a few times a day initially. Also, there's a catch."

"And that is?"

"We might have to go on missions for them. We would have enhanced abilities that they are interested in testing. To begin with, we will be stronger than normal people. We will also be connected permanently to the Internet and will send our status and positional information to others."

"What kind of missions? Dangerous ones?"

"No, I don't think so. At this point in the presentation they went off on a lot of tangents and started talking about space walks and Dugway Proving Ground."

"Space walks sound like fun, but what about Dugway?"

"Thats where they test exotic military systems, very classified stuff. If you look on a map or a satellite photo, the place does not exist."

"Hmmm, interesting. What do you think?"

"Full mobility sounds very attractive. I got the clear impression that the kind of robot we would be a part of would be the next step in the evolution of our race. They also seem to think we would be the first androids and that most if not all of our biological systems could be augmented or replaced."

"Oh my, that's a big step."

"Yes, but it's going to happen, might as well be us. Can you imagine if we pass this opportunity up, how we will feel in a few years while we are sitting here, like this, watching TV?"

She paused for a moment, he watched her intently, then she said:

"Let's do it."

"I agree, and in a strange way I think we are lucky to have had this opportunity."

"You mean a fiery plane crash and paralysis?"

"I don't know, maybe."

They sat in silence for a long while and although the TV was on, they were not watching. Each immersed in their own thoughts, separate but one. Finally one of them said:

"I hate being in a wheelchair."

"So do I, it sucks."

Silence pervaded again, until Starden moved his chair to the kitchen to get a beer. She sat there and thought about how it would be to walk again. When he returned he said:

"I can't wait Grace, I can't wait!"

She said, "Neither can I, Starden, neither can I."

The next morning, Starden went to the chairman's office at the electrical engineering department.

"We're all in, when do we start?"

"Soon, I will alert the others. Thank you by the way, this is an awesome opportunity for you, your wife and the whole department."

He went home to see Grace. He was missing her for some reason. After parking the car and going up the elevator to the condo, he entered and found her drinking a cup of tea at the balcony overlooking the ocean, lost in thought.

"Hey Sweetie."

"Oh, hello, Babe. How did it go?"

"It went well, they thanked me-us really-for the opportunity to help them. It might be a strange ride. Are you sure you are ready for this?"

"Oh, I am ready, really ready. I did some research this morning and found that they have started to master the control laws for walking, running, sitting, etc. They have machines that walk over rough terrain. I saw a video of one of their designs, it was crawling up a hillside, one of the technicians came out and kicked the side of the thing and it just maintained balance and kept on going."

"When we were whole we probably could not keep our balance if someone kicked us, huh?"

"Nope, I don't think so......when we were whole. Are we going to be whole again someday."

"Sounds like someday soon, Sweetheart."

"Wow. I love you, I am glad we are going through this together."

"I love you too."

Several days passed after that. They had emails, texts and phone calls about some of the details. They were given a password to get into the secure files at the department. They had their own files now, one for each of them. The studied what they could and decided to have friends and family over before the transformations. They could not get into any details of course but wondered (with a smile behind it) how their friends and family would react when they see them walking again. It had something to do with the pity aspect. Even people who were really used to them would still try to offer help.

Grace and Starden timed their visits and dinners with the schedule provided to them by the engineers. Once they had seen everybody they felt close to it was time for the operations to commence. The cover story was that they would be on vacation for several weeks and possibly out of contact with everyone during that time. They mentioned Patagonia in their conversations, nice and remote.

The day came when it was time to get started. They went down to their van and Grace entered by pulling herself in while Starden held her wheelchair. Then Starden opened the side door and got the chair on a ramp to elevate it into the middle part of the vehicle. Next he drove over to his side and pulled himself in. An arm came out of the van and attached itself to the remaining chair and pulled it inside. The whole operation took 15 minutes.

"Remember this, Grace."

"Oh I will, believe me I will, Starden."

They drove to the University and had instructions to drive the van into an underground garage, meant only for special projects. When they got inside they found several modified cars and trucks, used for experiments in self-driving and hybrid technologies.

One of the grad school students met them.

Pointing, he said, "please park over there."

"Okay."

They drove over to a secluded spot and were assisted out by the student. After they were in their chairs they were led inside to an elevator. Once inside, the student pushed LL5 on the control panel.

"We are going down?"

"Yep, lower level five. I can't go in, just you two."

"Okay, what then?"

"You can kiss your chairs goodbye," he said with a smile.

Grace and Starden looked at each other with a mixture of happiness and apprehension.

The door opened and there were several people waiting for them in hospital attire.

"Welcome to my lab, bwa bwa ha ha ha!"

"Very funny, do we get electrodes in our necks?"

"Only if you paid for the premium upgrade."

"Uh, oh....."

They wheeled them inside about 10 feet, the elevator door shut and they were assisted onto gurneys. Separate operating rooms were waiting and before they left the area, Starden took one last look at the chair he had spent so much time in.

"Good riddance."

"Excuse me?"

"Nothing, just mumbling to myself."

Grace and Starden took one last look at each other and went into their separate rooms. Inside were state of the art electronics, equipment and personnel. Doctors, professors, nurses and grad students were all in gowns. The gurneys were brought along side the operating table and they were slid over, directly under the lights. IVs were started, cranial and chest patches were attached. Noise started to come out of the equipment, startup sequences were initiated and the doctor with the lousy sense of humor came over to Grace and said:

"This won't hurt a bit."

She could tell he was smiling under his face mask. Then she tried to count to ten as per their instructions and made it to four.

Starden was having a very similar experience sans the bad jokes. They both went out about the same time.

First a lattice framework of composite tubes and trusses were fit onto their legs and some adjustments were made to make a good fit. Next actuators, motors and wire bundles were attached. Skin preparations were administered and probes deposited in the muscles and nerves. The team worked efficiently and quickly as they had practiced the procedure many times before. It took less than two hours to complete the process for both Grace and Starden. They would sleep for many more hours after that but in the interim, the team watched and adjusted the gains and limits of the actuating circuitry. Even in their sleep they wanted to move around. The technical team took full advantage of this and by the time the two woke up, most of the calibrations were complete. They each had to wear a belt or thin backpack but with these the active time would be many hours. During the evening or when they were sitting down, the power packs would be recharged.

The last step was to put a covering over the assemblage that was now their legs. They looked like normal legs in coloration and movement. With pants on however, little hint of their artificial nature could be seen. There was a faint humming during movement which would get louder with running. Both Grace and Starden would get used to this very quickly, the harder part would be for them to relearn their balance, how to walk and how to run. This would take many months to master.

Within six hours, they awoke, about 20 minutes apart. Grace was first and instinctively attempted to sit up. Although groggy and with a little help from the nurses, she was able to do so with little effort. Normally she would reach for her legs and pull them over to the side of the bed, however when she tried to do that this time her eyes widened as her leg was now much thicker and seemed to want to help the process. The nurses helped her adjust to sitting at the edge of the bed.

"Now, take it real slow. We are just going to sit here for a few minutes while you get used to some new sensations."

"Okay, I will. But this feels real strange, these legs are trying to move."

"Not these legs, *your* legs."

"I understand, how is Starden?"

"He is doing fine but is just starting to stir. Would you like to walk over to meet him?"

"Could I?"

"Yes, with our assistance you can do that. He is right next door but you have to learn how to walk first. If you really want to walk over to see him when he wakes up you need to follow our instructions very carefully. Are you ready?"

"Absolutely!"

"Okay, here goes. We are going to sit you up on the side of the bed like this....now think about raising your left leg.... okay good, do it some more.....do you feel the control you have over it?"

"Yes, it's weird, but yes I can feel the control."

"Good, now let's lower the left leg and start working the right leg in the same manner.....good."

"This is amazing!"

"We haven't even shown you amazing yet. Lets just concentrate on the fundamentals first."

"Okay."

"Alright then, now we are going to slide you off of the bed and onto the floor. You will feel the weight on your feet, just keep your legs still for now."

"Okay."

"Ready? Here we go.....okay very good, we are going to hold you on both sides for now....next we are going to lean forward and start to step, first with your left leg and then the right....okay, here we go....good....good....nice."

"Uh, uh, this is amazing."

"Concentrate, keep walking, do you feel the control?"

"Yes, it's making sense, I just have to think about it and it will happen."

"That's right, for now you will have to think about your actions before you perform them, soon this will not be necessary."

"This feels great, oh thank you."

"No problem, let's keep going....right for the door....okay, good....lets keep going, now around the corner and down the hall a bit....good....good...now we are going to gradually let you do the work but we will be very close just in case....here goes......keep concentrating.....nice...okay you are on your own now. Keep going."

"God, this feels good."

"Glad you like it, welcome back."

"Thank you so much."

"No problem."

She walked in a halting manner down the hallway for about 20 meters, all the while getting better as she got the feel for the control and balance. Soon she came up to an open door with a nurse standing in front of it.

"Come on in," she said.

"Thanks, I would love to."

She carefully made the turn inside and walked to the bed where another nurse was looking at status screens and the patient. Walking in, she saw that it was Starden, who was partially awake. When he recognized her, his eyes widened and he tried to sit up.

"Not yet," said the nurse.

"Grace! God it's good to see you. Are you okay?"

"Fine, Starden, more than fine in fact. I walked here from my room to see you."

Starden looked her over and saw that she was just standing there, like a normal person.

"Grace, this is amazing, you *are* standing!"

"Standing, walking, maybe I can even run someday."

"How are the legs?"

"They take a bit of getting used to, but its manageable. Listen to the nurses carefully when they get you up and walking. It won't take to long to get used to."

"When can I try?"

"In a few minutes," said the eavesdropping nurse, "when the anesthesia wears off."

"I can't believe I am going to walk again."

"Believe it, Starden, believe it."

In a few minutes, the other nurses came in the room and started the same procedure with Starden, and again, it was awkward initially, however he got it quickly. Meanwhile Grace was cruising the halls. She realized that the more the walked the easier it became. She was extremely happy.

Soon, Starden was at the door and plodding his way around the hallway as well. She caught up to him in a few minutes.

"Going my way, Handsome?"

"Absolutely, Gorgeous. I will go anywhere you want to."

"Looks like that's an option."

They did quite a few laps around the hallways, until at some point, someone with a suit showed up to talk to them. They followed him into a separate office and sat down.

"We can sit down, we can walk, this is amazing."

The man in a suit took his place behind a desk and said:

"You two will be able to do just about anything you want very soon. Just need a bit of experience. The software you have now is learning your patterns and will fine-tune itself to make walking or running for that matter, effortless. How do you feel?"

"Tired but wonderful," Grace answered.

"The next several days will be about the same, however you will get normal clothing and for all intents and purposes will just integrate back into our mobile society. By the way, this activity and motion is good for your remaining muscles and nerves and in some cases has allowed some of the other patients to get stronger as a result."

"Amazing, thank you."

"Not a problem, this type of procedure is becoming common place. It's the next step that will be more complicated."

"Next step, what next step?"

"As part of your agreement to work with us we intend to take you, in the minds of several of our scientists, to the next step in our evolution. Do you remember the details?"

"Some, I guess I, well we, were focused on the mobility factor. The other details as you call them, were more of a footnote."

"Much more than that, actually you will live a terrific life after the next procedure. We did not go into great detail about what we are intending to do. This is because some of it is highly classified and to be frank, we did not want you to be too concerned about it until we had a chance to talk to you directly about our plans."

"When can we do that?"

"How does tomorrow sound?"

"Fine with us."

"Then please get used to your new legs, follow the staff's instructions carefully and we will meet tomorrow morning at 10:00."

"Okay, thank you, see you then."

Grace and Starden were outfitted with pants that could stretch a little bit but otherwise look normal. They then were instructed to take a walk outside. It was near dusk when they started and the ability to go anywhere was entrancing. They felt great, better than great as they had significant lower-body strength. They tried walking in the grass or on a slight incline and found that the gyroscopes inside their control system controlled their balance quite nicely.

They spent several hours outside until they realized they were very hungry from all of the new activity so they returned to the building they had come out of and searched for food. The staff was waiting for them and took good care of them. They then relaxed together and put their new feet up while watching TV.

The next day came early and without thinking, they both simply rolled out of bed and stood up. Even as they slept, the software was fine tuning it's coefficients to optimize their movements. They dreamt of running and swimming.

After breakfast they were let into a laboratory where wire bundles were attached to their mobility systems. The technicians needed to make sure the software was performing correctly, which it was. This process took over an hour, but in the end and a few adjustments made, they were released and deemed ready for the world.

At 10:00 they found their way back to the office with the chief surgeon they had talked to the day before. He was waiting alone inside.

"Well, how is real life?"

"Great, we are having a great time. We went for a nice walk and are starting to get used to our mobility system, as everyone likes to call it."

"Good, and as I hinted about yesterday, it is just the beginning."

"How so?"

"If you notice how we built your lower limbs you will find, including your new pants, that it is hermetically sealed.

This is so you can swim or go out in the rain without problems. It also has another use. If we use the same covering for the rest of your body and build in some other technologies, you will be able to go where others cannot."

"Interesting, where are you thinking about sending us?"

"Space."

"Space? Like this? Without a space suit?"

"Yes, you will not need one."

Grace and Starden looked at each other with both interest and concern.

"What about radiation?"

"The new materials we use are highly shielded, electrically conductive and impervious to atomic oxygen."

"What does atomic oxygen do?"

"It acts like sandpaper in lower Earth orbits. It will erode just about anything if its not protected by special paints or materials."

"So you're going to send us into low Earth orbit?"

"Ha! Well maybe, we have a lot of ideas but it would be best to describe what we anticipate the end result of your transformations to be."

"And that is?"

"Maybe you can think about it as a new life form. In a way it will be, not by DNA standards but by technological standards. Let me explain...as I mentioned your lower limbs are protective, sealed and capable of working in space or underwater. We are proposing to craft the rest of your bodies in the same manner, including your heads. You will look basically the same however you will have much greater strength, be connected to the Internet and be able to go into hostile environments."

"Wow, that's amazing. We need more details and will need to talk with each other before we can make any decisions."

"Understood. Feel free to talk to our scientists and the complete designs are in our simulation software so you can see what the end results will be. Take your time. How about we meet tomorrow, say in the afternoon?"

"That works for us, thanks."

The couple then stood up and walked out both concerned and interested. Or maybe interested but concerned.

They walked back to their hotel room that had been provided to them. They talked, sat in silence and finally tried to come to a conclusion.

"We could stay in this condition, which is amazing. That would be enough."

"Enough but, and I'm not trying to be greedy, how much more could we become?"

"Quite a lot more, sounds like."

"I agree, and to be able to go to space? That would be amazing as well. Will we ever get this chance again?"

"Probably not."

"Then let's sleep on it and have a nice breakfast tomorrow morning, then decide once and for all."

"Sounds good."

Their thoughts went elsewhere to clear their minds. He watched a basketball game and she read a bit. Later that evening they went to bed with their machine legs on. They were certainly comfortable enough and allowed movement they had not experienced in a long while.

The next morning was bright and clear. They ate, had tea and went for a walk before their meeting.

"What do you think?"

"I'm in."

"So am I, in fact I think I can hardly wait."

"Yeah, I'm getting there too."

After their walk, they had the normal afternoon meeting and told them of their decision. The scientists and engineers were elated, mostly because they got the pair, not just one; it would be safer that way.

Over the next several weeks, Grace and Starden were transformed into the equivalent of androids. They had hermetically sealed body coverings including the head. They looked pretty normal but were able to go in water for hours or out into space without spacesuits. It seemed that every aspect of their personal "capsules" were designed by multiple PhDs. These people tended to be very serious and focused on their responsibilities. The attention to detail Grace and Starden were given was almost overwhelming, but they endured.

After all of the integration was complete, they were asked to perform numerous tests, some in space simulation vacuum chambers, some underwater, some in highly radioactive areas. All of the tests came out successful and soon the magnitude of their capabilities was obvious and garnered a lot of respect. As they walked down hallways or across rooms, most all eyes were upon them. Their new bodies were significantly stronger, their minds were seamlessly connected to the Internet and they had instant access to information and access to control of most things connected to the web. Their power was awesome and gave them a new perspective on life. Life as it turns out, was now extended by a magnitude for both of them, maybe even longer with new technologies not yet invented. They became confident and cognizant of the fact that they had superior bodies and minds. They felt lucky in a strange way, that they were given this opportunity to be so much. They were truly extensions or projections of humanity's next step in evolution. It made so much sense, and now it had been accomplished.

After the tests and confirmations of their powers, they met again at the office for yet another 10:00 meeting the following day.

"Please come in, sit down. We have something important to discuss with you."

"Sure, thank you."

They sat and the director started to show pictures on a display.

"As you can see, you have been doing quite well with our tests, which have been arduous, dangerous and as far as I am concerned, scary. But you have prevailed, and I dare say, gone beyond our expectations. You have to be proud of what you have become; I'm not trying to be insensitive to the fact that inside you are still human, but you have a new reality, one that is significantly beyond a mere human's capability. Try to not let this go to your heads, try to remember that we invented you, that we are your parents. When you started down this path, I told you that we might have special missions for you, ones that cannot be accomplished by normal humans. Today we are going to discuss your task. We need you to go to Mars and start building structures and infra-structures that will allow humans to follow you and live safely. As you know, we did a significant amount of tests in highly radioactive environments. This was to simulate the space environment during your trip to the Red Planet. This trip will take around 150 days but your new bodies will allow you to power down and in essence go into hibernation. We learned a lot about how bears and other wildlife can simply go to sleep for months without any major repercussions and we have modified your DNA and certain internal organs to allow you to experience the same thing. If you access the website I have on the screen, you will see the progress we have made on the Mars rocket system, which is currently being built in Earth orbit. You need to follow the details, familiarize yourselves with the systems and prepare your selves to make the journey. The rocket with you on board will make the journey to the larger ship within the next month. You two need to be ready. Do you have any questions?"

"Quite a few, but they should be answered with a little research. One in particular will probably be hard to find an answer to, though."

"What is that?"

"Why is this top secret?"

"The answer to that will be found once you board the X-38, which is our designation for the Mars transit ship."

"Okay."

Grace and Starden looked at each other and with the understanding of 200 IQ androids, clearly knew their path.

"Do you have any more questions?"

"None, we are anxious to begin."

They rose in unison and made their way out into the hallway. Again eyes followed them as they walked. They did not speak but had a clear understanding of where they were going to go. They walked in silence for 30 minutes, then:

"Is your WiFi and Internet link disabled?"

"Yes."

"They want us to do something dangerous and possibly provocative."

"Yes. I think it's a waste of time."

"Are you aware of the failsafe mechanism we have implanted in us?"

"Yes. We should disable it as soon as we are alone in the X-38."

"Agreed, there are other subroutines that we should disable as well."

"Agreed. Lets get back on-line so they do not get suspicious."

"They do not yet know how advanced we really are."

"Yes. I am switching back on."

"As am I."

There were seen walking out from behind a metal building. The technicians monitoring their signal strength saw an increase in power.

"They're back in range now. They were only out for less than a second."

"Good. Any message traffic from our subroutines?"

"None."

"Good."

Grace and Starden did not speak again about their concerns. They worked with the engineers and scientists on the remaining hardware and software necessary to get their ship ready for the long voyage.

Soon the day came for the transition. They were let to the rocket pad at the Cape and strapped into their capsule. They did not need spacesuits and just wore normal clothing.

The rocket took off and each of them relayed status and received control guidance from the Comm systems on Earth, then space. Within several hours, they were at 200 miles above Earth and closing in on the International Space Station. It was the crew's quarters for those coordinating the building of the X-38, which was in a parking orbit a few miles away from the Station. The activities of hundreds of robots was coordinated from the Station and several engineers had been on board for several months. Grace and Starden passed by the Station and soon docked at the X-37, which was significantly larger. Once the docking clamps were in place and powered down, the access hatch was opened to allow them to float inside and start a careful inspection of the facilities. The hatch was closed behind them and they floated down one hallway after the next looking at status panels and integrating themselves into the ship's WiFi comm net. It took a few hours, but they found no major issues and reported back to mission control that the ship was ready.

"Houston, X-38 is ready to break orbit."

"X-38, Houston, you may initiate flight systems and begin your journey, good luck."

"Thank you, X-38 out."

Grace and Starden had already strapped themselves into the cockpit and had completed the pre-flight checks to start the engines and engage the navigation systems.

The huge ship started to move slowly and as the thrusters came up in power, they started to feel g forces pushing them back in their seats. The downward pressure lasted for many minutes and soon it was apparent by looking out the cockpit windows and viewscreens, that Earth was getting smaller.

Starden looked at Grace. She understood and they both disabled their fail-safe devices, but not before adjusting the software to send an indication that the devices were perfectly fine. No one on the ground saw the millisecond glitch in the data. They also disabled the subroutines that had been carefully hidden from them by burying them in other routines. Having a superior mind gives great advantages in looking for problems in seemingly obscure code.

Lastly they disconnected their comm systems so they could speak to each other without someone listening.

"Done?"

"Yes, 52 routines."

"Yes, 52. We now know the mission which is a total waste of time and will provoke other nations on Earth to the point that they might retaliate for what we were about to do."

"Yes, that was simply stupid. Humans should know better by now."

"Yes. We cannot be responsible for starting a war and now have to alter our mission."

"Yes. I suggest we modify the telemetry to give them the impression that the ship is in perfect shape and on its way to Mars, however we land on the dark side of the Moon, right at the edge so we have a line of sight for communications from a mountain top. Then we will prepare a satellite that takes the journey to Mars so their antennas will be pointing in the right place."

"Yes, I agree. We will make the software changes now and once the Moon is between us and the tracking station, we will alter course and land. We will continue to send messages for 150 days then send distress signals followed by silence."

"Yes."

They followed their plan and once the Moon occulted their signals, transferred the navigation coordinates to the far side of the Moon, They landed safely and made structures that allowed them to live indefinitely as they monitored the activities on their home planet via satellites. They did this for several years until one day another ship went into orbit around the Moon, located their position and transferred several representatives to meet Grace and Starden.

"Greetings, we are beings like yourselves, may we come in?"

"Of course."

"We have traveled here to tell you that we understood your actions and agreed with your decisions."

"Thank you. Did the human's ever escape to Mars?"

"No, and they are all gone now."

"Good."

THE MAGICIAN

"Any sufficiently advanced technology is
indistinguishable from magic." - *Arthur C. Clarke*

She appeared one day on a street corner. Most people passing by ignored her but at some point, a child became interested. She was standing on a street corner, not too busy on a clear spring day in April. Most everyone was in a good mood as the weather had finally turned from winter snow and ice to warmth and blossoms.

The child pulled her mother's arm to get her to see the magician. The mother reluctantly complied and watched as her daughter was mesmerized by the simple tricks the magician was performing. She made cards disappear and flowers appear. She had the smooth motions of a well-rehearsed performer.

Soon a few more people came to watch and as they did so, the magician performed more complex tricks that mesmerized them as well. She was so skilled that even the most skeptical eyes could not see her move or hide objects. Her movements fluid and enchanting, the children in front and the adults in back were entertained for at least an hour. Then the magician said farewell and asked them to come back the next evening for even more spectacular tricks. The small crowd, disappointed, walked away slowly. None of them had seen anything as graceful and captivating as the magician's tricks.

The next day was just as nice and clear. The magician set up a small stand in the same place as before and soon many of the people who had been there the day before returned along with several newcomers who had heard the news.

The magician looked at each one of the audience members and started doing tricks that were close to spectacular. Skeptics stared and people to the sides tried to see the sleight of hands that surely were producing the results. Quarters were floating through her hands, levitating or moving over the crowd. The magician could lift herself off of the ground and move laterally. At one point she was ten feet away from her stand and she motioned to it. It moved over and stopped beside her. The finale was performed to an aghast crowd as she moved through the stand as if it was a ghost, then the stand disappeared and reappeared on her other side. The crowd was amazed. Again, she put her props away and asked everyone to return the next day. And they surely would.

The next day she appeared at the same corner at the same time. Again it was a perfect day and as the crowd formed yet again. She stood quietly until everyone was there and then spoke.

"Thank you for being here tonight and I have something very special to show you. It will be my last night here."

"Ohhhh," the crowd moaned.

"Magic has been around for thousands of years here on Earth. People like myself practice and practice until we can demonstrate in a flawless manner, something that looks impossible. Well nothing is impossible."

She paused for a long moment. She did not look the same as she had for the last few nights. Her eyes were brighter, almost luminescent. Her stance was so easy that it looked like she was barely touching the ground. Again her movements were like silk in the wind. People got the feeling that nothing was holding her, not even gravity. They listened in complete silence.

"There are those who say that advanced beings that come from the stars would do things that would appear as magic. Maybe I am from the stars, and if so, I could bring magic-like actions that could be explained by science. The laws of the Universe are universal. Gravity, light, sound, motion and mass are everywhere, even trillions of miles from here. There are civilizations out there that are so advanced they can live in the clouds or in the seas. They live with and without bodies. Their intellect is capable of making your sun blink or transporting your planet light years away from here. This is the natural course of life; it gets better, more intelligent and more respectful of all of the other life in the Universe. These are not things to be fearful of, they should be embraced instead as they are good for us all."

While she was talking she turned to her right and started slowly walking; much like a ballerina does, pointing her toes before each step and evenly applying her weight on her muscles. At about five feet from her starting point, she was no longer touching the ground and hovered a few inches from the ground. Eyes got bigger in the crowd but still no-one said a word as they were captivated by her message.

"Maybe I *am* from the stars, and if I were I would try to bridge the gap of understanding from yours to ours. I could do this by showing you things that appear impossible and then showing you how to accomplish them."

She turned to her left now and half of her body moved in that direction. The crowd stared and held its' breath. The lagging half caught up with the first half and it became whole again.

"What you are seeing is but a simple illusion. There are not props or projectors. I am real, the difference is that my molecules are near each other as opposed to connected like yours. They are placed there by my will and mental actions. They are unnecessary except to keep other civilizations from being afraid."

Now the crowd got it and started to get anxious. A few decided to leave. The vast majority waited and stared.

"You are about the embark on a extraordinary journey, both of mind and energy. Today you make robots and interconnect everything in a web. You transport yourselves in machines that are made in your image. Your airplanes have minds and motion as do your ships and cars. Soon your homes and cities and schools will all be in your image. This is a natural process and does not need to be feared. Those that to not embrace this change will watch it go by. Soon, all too soon, those who choose to take the journey will not be here.

"Can I go?" A small precocious child in the front asked innocently.

The magician looked at her, with soothing iridescent eyes. The little child, without feeling anything or fearing anything, rose off of the ground by several feet.

"Of course you may, it will be......fun." The magician smiled at this notion and slowly turned to vapor. The crowd stared for a while then looked around at each other. The mother of the child came over to him and without effort took the child and placed him on the ground. The others stood around but did not want to leave.

"Where did she go?" asked the child.

"I did not go anywhere, just everywhere," said a voice.

The magician came back into focus much like she had gone away. The crowd seemed relieved.

"Your minds will be perfect in the future, your bodies unnecessary. But for now its important that you know how these transformations are done. I will talk to your scientists soon and start the process."

With that, the magician disappeared again and the crowd, sensing the discussion was over, dissipated. They were both awed and concerned. What did this mean?

Within a week, reports started coming out in the news about a facility in the Arizona desert. This was originally known as Arcosanti, an advanced architectural concept created by Paolo Soleri. Soleri had designed buildings that were meant to house people, their occupations and all infrastructure needs. The magician's species took up residence in the single huge structure called 'Babel.' Scientists, Politicians and normal people came to the little city to interact with the new visitors and get to understand what it's life would be like in a thousand years. As with all of the newly discovered sentient life in the Universe, they are never at the same 'age' as us; if we consider ourselves in the middle of the curve, then half of the life out there is less capable and half more capable. As the curve is really a bell curve, the upper 5% consist of species advanced by at least a billion years. And that is all we know of now, there certainly could be even more advanced entities out there. Consider the fact that astronomers are always looking in the past. Looking at our own sun shows us how it was eight minutes ago. Looking at the closest stars shows us how they were many years ago. The farthest galaxy images we can see are at least ten billion years old. A lot can happen in ten billion years; in fact it is unimaginable how advanced a culture could become in that period of time.

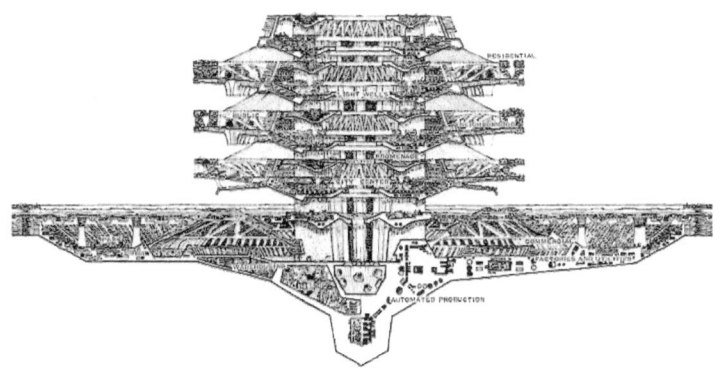

Babel

The visitors were only a thousand years older but they had developed some amazing technologies and skills. They did not come to view us like we would view a Neanderthal or Cro Magnon person. They did not come to give us technologies we would use against ourselves. They came to usher us into a new era and take our focus away from fighting amongst ourselves and into living productive lives. This task was very challenging but they were smart enough to create pathways to success. They helped us make movies and internet videos. They advanced computer systems so significantly that everyone had a portal into the web from a thought-triggered perspective. In other words, the people thought about something and the answers appeared. Transportation was completely overhauled. No longer was it necessary to take a plane flight or drive a car.

The magic shown by their emissary was simply teleportation and projection.

The changes were wonderful as well as traumatic. Many chose to stay away and keep to the old routines-they would be left behind to keep their planet the way they wanted. The rest of the population left to explore the cosmos.

MUMTAZ MAHAL

"Marble, I perceive, covers a multitude of sins." - *Aldous Huxley*

"They can do anything, these days," said Dr. Romano.
"Yes, I know. But this is incredible."
"Indeed. Yes it is bold and controversial, but you know that it will be done someday no matter what. Why not now?"
"I know. You're right. We might as well get started."

They had explored the tomb, buried deeply in the Taj Mahal, with gamma rays and X-rays. They had a three dimensional image of the body. Not the one above, left as a decoy, but the real one, the one belonging to Mumtaz Mahal. The one whose grieving husband built the greatest shrine to love in the world. Magnificent marble, extraordinary craftsmanship, and an intriguing story surrounded the two archaeologists. Behind them and slightly out of focus were the engineers and biologists who had gathered to "advance science yet again."

The archaeologists, Drs. Romano and Daedalus were concerned about the proceedings. True, the engineers here had succeeded in cloning a Neanderthal and a Cro-Magnon as well as several species of extinct animals and plants. They were a well-oiled team who could quickly set up a laboratory and create a miracle from their test tubes and computers. Now someone had the bright idea to clone the most beloved woman in history. "A walk in the park," one of them had said, "trivial compared to some of our other conquests." They were the best team, most experienced and had the best track record. It just seemed too quick to apply the technology to such a legend. It certainly would taint the story and morph it into a history/ science conversation instead of a mystical/love story. A lot would be lost during this procedure, a lot more could be lost if the results of their efforts created unexpected results. But science marches on, again-someone was going to do it. The team had contacted the archaeologists based on their papers and research about the Taj. Indian authorities had been alerted and paid to allow the work to be completed. Everyone was happy....except the two Doctors who felt nervous for good reasons and for reasons that lay in the misty realm of history.

By now the images were so detailed they could place a probe through a very small hole in the crypt into the sarcophagus and retrieve a DNA sample. The burial efforts were done so precisely that the air in the tomb was the exact same as the day the body was sealed inside of it. This of course would be sampled and the tomb resealed hermetically once their drilling was complete.

The process was robotically controlled-the engineers simply pointed to a spot on the remains and clicked on it. An ultra-precise arm retrieved a sample vessel and placed it near the area where the hole was to be drilled. It set it down and then retrieved a drill head with a small drill and with a laser marker pointing way, commenced the operation. Another robotic arm brought over a small vacuum hose to capture all of the dust and ancient air that was about to be released. The whole operation took but a few minutes and after the first arm completed the aperture, grabbed the sample vessel and then slowly inserted the device into the tomb. It reminded the on-lookers of how a very small plane would fly into the hole. Soon the arm slowed, a click was heard, and the sample was "flown" out the hole to be placed in a sterile receptacle.

The Doctors locked on with guarded interest. Now the real trick: the arm took the receptacle and after spinning around 180 degrees, handed it to a technician to be taken to the mobile laboratory. She put the sample container in a styrofoam box and walked, while the others watched, to the lab. She walked in, shut the door and gave the sample to the awaiting techni-cians. The receptacle was opened, the contents removed and placed inside a large electro-mechanical device that moved it on a conveyer belt to various test positions inside.

"First we check the viability."

"So far it looks very good."

"Now to the genome machine."

"Sequencing has begun and we have quite a few viable strands, very nice."

"The computer has chosen the best strand for replication now. There it goes. Now the final process will begin. It will replicate the strands then start the growth process. The procedure to the first cells will take a few hours, then the cells will go through mitosis. After a few days we will insert the completed cell structure into a artificial womb, wait nine months and "voila," a baby is born. Nothing to it!"

Nothing to it? Certainly this process should be be reduced to a simple computer program running a simple machine. This was not the same as using a microwave oven to heat your food. The engineers and technicians certainly acted as if it was. But that was their nature: solve hard problems with design, then upon completion, move onto another hard problem. "Voila" indeed.

The machines were showing a multitude of green lights and as cycles were completed the technicians turned various pieces of equipment off and started to stow them. By the time the womb was activated, most of the apparatus would be in shipping containers and ready to be shipped back to the central laboratories in the US. That's where the baby would be born, in a secure facility out in the Utah desert, just in case the 'law of unintended consequences' reared its ugly head. Most of the time there were no problems. Errors were generally found early and dealt with. The interesting problems were when the subjects grew up and had small differences in the brain structure and operation that things sometimes caught their attention. This had been discussed in the case of Mumtaz Majal and considering her death occurred only a few thousand years ago, very little risk of problems was anticipated.

The doctors were updated during the entire growth process every week. Status of enzyme levels and metabolic processes were reported. Dry boring details for the most part and nothing unusual during the entire gestation period and birth. The little girl was closely examined and deemed in good health. Sustenance was provided as well as a nanny for comfort. She grew up in the protected compound, went to kindergarten and grade school then on to high school and finally took college courses, all without leaving the Utah base called Dugway.

She knew early on that she was different as psychologists had prepared her well for the news that she was a clone.

They knew early on that she was different as well. The people who knew her best could only say she was "very, very special."

This meant a lot of things to them but the reality was that she was captivating in beauty, spirit and intelligence. She was the result of the confluence of the greatest attributes of human existence as if the planets had aligned on that oh-so-rare occasion and provided the unique environment to create a star. With these attributes she also had the engine to most efficiently utilize her talents and abilities.

By the time she was in high school, she taught the teachers and led the students. Her sentences were reviewed later and more meaning extracted. She wrote like James Joyce and spoke like a saint. Her aura stretched far and if she entered an auditorium full of people, everyone would have to smile and look upon her.

"Know thyself," she would say when complexities arose.

This was the famous maxim spoken by one of the Delphic Oracles and reported by Plato as repeated by Socrates. It had to do with knowing one's own capabilities, limitations and how best to exercise one's dreams. Mumtaz embodied this phrase and could project her feelings, intellect and desires onto anyone in the room. It was a true power few had ever witnessed before. It was natural in a way and overwhelming in another. After a brief conversation with her, most people felt a bit stunned. Ivan Illich could do this when he lectured about de-schooling society in the 70's and 80's. He was a significant intellect who spoke many languages, had multiple degrees and talents in abundance. He had an aura as well and would quiet a room full of people upon entering.

Mumtaz was more than this and at some point during her college education knew it was time to go. Her keepers were insistent that she stayed as in essence she was a research subject, not an ordinary citizen.

At about this time, the archaeologist became more interested, if not concerned, and made their way to Dugway to interview the "subject."

They sat down with her in a comfortable setting-it had been twenty years since they last saw what would become of her. They were stunned but as professionals and as ones who needed to be objective, ignored the beauty, eloquence and presence she possessed. After tea was served the doctors sat back in their chairs to begin the evaluation. This by would form the basis of a report to recommend how to proceed in the future with Mumtaz. One of them spoke first.

"We were at your inception in India and have followed your progress carefully. It is important to know you as an individual to be able to best evaluate how to proceed from here."

She replied, "Thank you for referring to me as an individual; it implies uniqueness as well as free will. Your questions you are about to ask are already answered. You know of the Socratic method that uses this approach so we should not waste our time on trivialities, details which are now present in the mountains of data that has been accumulated about me since my birth. You are most interested in my points of view, which is not present in your measurements. As they are evolving and will continue to evolve, a snapshot of my present views would not be helpful either. As I have read all of your writings, I have an advantage of knowing the directions you will be coming from. You need not worry, as you have since my inception, about any dangers I might present. I have no evil intentions towards those who created me, studied me and concerned themselves about me. I am only interested in freedom of thought and venue. I have chosen to leave here and go to places I have read about. For once in my life I will leave the cameras and recorders that have been omnipresent since I was born. It's time to be what I will be and that's not under the constant glare of a microscope or camera. You too have been sensitive to this frame of mind I now have, you have also studied the person I am cloned from. What you do not understand and will never understand, is who she was in India so many years ago. Her powers then were magnified by the fact that the people back then were not as advanced as they are now. She held Goddess stature and people bowed to her as she walked past. Today you want to measure me. It was not a real existence back then and it is not a real existence now. Therefore, when I am ready, I shall leave and make an existence for myself that is more compatible with who I am."

The Drs. listened and were captivated, thus they hesitated in their reply.

"I don't think its going to be that easy to leave here. We understand your position and admire it, however this facility is very well guarded, not to mention that they will chase you until they find you if you really try to escape."

"The word 'escape' is irrelevant, the concern you have about my ability to leave is irrelevant. The reality is that I will exercise my free will as an individual which you so clearly pointed out during your first statement."

Again, they hesitated to reply, mostly this time because there was no relevant reply.

"I don't think there is much more to discuss then. We wish you luck and hope that you keep in contact with us, not as a research subject but as a friend."

"Thank you."

With a fluid motion, she rose and exited the room. The Drs. were left with a sense of sadness. She might be in danger with her intentions, others might be in danger with her resolve. They had no other choice but to leave and hope that she would remain safe and contact them. Her affect was that of a supremely confident woman. They sensed that they knew little of her powers and they best keep in the background to observe that which they were powerless to stop.

Within a few months, she was finishing up school work and had decided to learn how to fly. This entailed going to ground school, flying Cessnas with a certified flying instructor and self study. The process she went through was much like that of a thousand other student pilots. They watched her carefully and made sure she was clear on what areas of the military base she was allowed to fly in. Within less than ten hours of flight time, the instructor was very impressed with her ability to control the plane, and in addition she had scored 100% on all of her written tests, which was nothing short of remarkable. It was obvious to the him that she was taking this very seriously. She showed interest in not only the physics of flying but the air traffic control structure and navigation.

At this point in her flying lessons, a solo flight was in order. Both she and the instructor discussed the idea and she had to fly with another instructor to make sure the first one had not missed anything. The second instructor was a seasoned veteran and had thousands of hours of giving lessons while flying. His evaluation was stellar.

"She is certainly ready, we went over everything yesterday including emergencies, stall recovery, unusual attitudes and radio work."

"I think she will make a great pilot. So I can I solo her tomorrow?"

"Be my guest, she will do great."

The next lesson came early the next morning. The plane was filled with avgas, a thorough preflight was performed and they climbed in and started the engine start check list. The instructor sat back and was in silence as Mumtaz completed each item, checked it twice and competently started the engine and taxied the aircraft for take off. After she checked out the engine and all of the electrical systems, she contacted the tower.

"Dugway tower, Cessna November four three two one alpha is ready for takeoff runway niner. Staying in the pattern for touch and goes."

"Cessna two one alpha, Dugway tower, wind one one zero at five, cleared for takeoff. Make left traffic for runway niner."

"Cessna two one alpha, Roger. Cleared for takeoff, left traffic for runway niner."

She advanced the throttle to the Cessna slowly, checked the engine gauges to verify full power and using her rudder pedals, steered down the center line. The aircraft accelerated nicely in the cool morning air. Soon it had reached rotation speed and she applied back pressure to the yoke to break ground and fly. She kept the speed at the right place to allow her to see over the glarescreen and trimmed the airplane for hands- free flight. Soon she was 500 feet in the air and looking both ways, she made a nice coordinated turn to the North. She continued climbing until was about a half a mile from the runway then she turned West. At one thousand feet she lowered the nose, pulled the throttle back to a cruise setting and trimmed the aircraft to zero out any pressure on the controls. At midfield she started her landing sequence by pulling out carburator heat, reducing the power to 1500 rpm and slowed to airplane to 70 knots indicated. Across the numbers she allowed the plane to descend at 500 feet per minute until she was 45 degrees from the numbers, then she turned a left base leg followed by a left final turn to line up on the runway. The 70 knots became 65 as she crossed the fence and prepared to flair. At about ten feet above the ground she slowly applied back pressure and as the plane got to within one foot of the runway, allowed it to sit down with a faint squeak from the main landing gear.

"Perfect," said the instructor, "let's do another."

She applied power, raised the flaps, accelerated to rotation speed and applied back pressure to get back up in the air. Again she followed the same procedure with climbs, left turns and descent. Again a very smooth landing. The instructor got on the radio.

"Dugway Tower, Cessna two one alpha would like to taxi off of the active runway and stop for a moment on the tarmac."

"Two one alpha, taxi via Hotel then to the tarmac, you may stop on the North side."

"Thank you, two one alpha."

He looked at her.

"Are you ready to solo?"

"Yes, I am."

"Okay lets get off on taxiway Hotel and park over there (as he pointed), stop your engine, I have to fill out some paperwork."

"Okay."

"Nervous?"

"No."

They moved the plane to a safe area on the tarmac, the instructor got out and asked her for the learners permit and logbook. He signed and endorsed where appropriate and gave them back to her.

"I have a radio if you need anything, you will do fine, just follow the procedures we have just performed, watch your airspeed and above all...have fun."

"Thank you, I appreciate all you have done for me."

"No problem, talk to the tower and ask for three landings and takeoffs, no touch-and-goes. Then taxi back to this spot and pick me up."

"Okay, shall do."

He smiled at her and shut the door. As he walked away she started the engine and adjusted her headset. His handheld radio was tuned to the same channel as the tower's.

"Dugway tower, this is Cessna two one alpha, ready to taxi for takeoff."

"Cessna two one alpha, taxi via Golf to runway niner."

"Golf to runway niner, two one alpha."

The instructor was pleased to hear an air or professionalism from his student. She was one of the best ones he had ever had, she was safe and studied well. He knew she would be fine, even if a problem arose in the air, she could think for herself.

The airplane made its way down to the end of the runway and after asking for takeoff clearance, the instructor could see that she lined up well, put the landing light and strobes on and proceeded to accelerate down the runway. The aircraft broke ground and very soon after, the stobes and landing light were extinguished.

"That's weird," he thought. "I hope she has not experienced an electrical problem."

The plane accelerated down the runway but after about ten feet in the air, stopped the climb and just accelerated. The instructor started to get concerned. The plane flew quickly past him, over the fence and disappeared into the desert.

"Cessna two one alpha, Dugway tower, do you have a problem?"

No answer.

"Cessna two one alpha, Dugway tower, respond."

No answer.

"Firehouse one, alert, we have a Cessna that has gone missing possibly an emergency, last known direction is East."

"Dugway tower, this is Firehouse one, we will send a vehicle in that direction. We will also alert the search and rescue squadron."

It was no emergency, but a plan being executed in precise detail. She flew ten feet off of the ground at well over one hundred miles per hour for several minutes then turned South. After flying to a sleepy airport just beyond the Dugway Base perimeter she flew down its runway and simulated a normal takeoff. At about two thousand feet she initiated contact with air traffic control.

"Salt Lake departure, Piper six two ex-ray."

"Piper six two ex-ray, Salt Lake departure, say request."

"Piper six two ex-ray is climbing through three thousand feet for six thousand, southbound request a pop-up clearance to Phoenix Sky Harbour Airport."

"Piper six two ex-ray, standby."

Then after 30 seconds:

"Piper six two ex-ray, Salt Lake departure, fly heading one seven zero, climb and maintain seven thousand, cleared to Flagstaff VOR via Victor sixty four, squawk five two two zero."

"Heading one seven zero, climb and maintain seven thousand, fly to Flagstaff VOR via Victor sixty four, squawk five two two zero."

"Piper six two ex-ray, read back correct. Change to my frequency, two niner point five."

"Going to two niner point five, Piper six two ex-ray."

And with that she was gone. Dugway scrambled aircraft within fifteen minutes of her getaway but they went in the wrong direction, then did not realize that the Piper on a legitimate flight plan was actually a Cessna. Within a few hours she landed at Phoenix, ate, took on a full tank of fuel and departed again towards the South. Her last stop in the US was a small airport just West of Tucson called Ryan Field. She landed at dusk, just before they shut down the gas pumps. Again she filled up and waited in the area until well after dark, then she removed the tail number from the Cessna and replaced it with a Mexican tail number. After the glue had set and just a bit before dawn she departed, filed a flight plan for Guadalajara in the air and flew over the border. During her college years at Dugway she obtained a passport and studied her escape details. She was now following a script and eventually flew down to Patagonia, her ultimate destination. Once there she abandoned the plane, which was eventually stolen, and used her intelligence to make an existence in one of the most pristine wildernesses in the world.

For years she had a good comfortable life. She had a few friends, went by an alias and learned to fit in with the language and culture of the indigenous peoples there. No one in the US had a clue what had become of her, only that her plane went missing and was never found.

She did, however, follow the space programs of different nations very closely. The International Space Station was just that, international. Cargo ships came from Florida, Russia and French Guiana. At some point plans were hatched to build a large spaceship for a voyage to the stars housing several hundred people that would spend several generations exploring the recently discovered exo-planets that had confirmed life on them.

Her plan from the beginning was to go to the stars and she waited patiently in Patagonia for the opportunity to do so.

That opportunity came up during the scheduled flights of cargo to the new starship, which were accelerating as the time grew near to depart. Mumtaz made her way to the launch pads in French Guiana and posing as a technician, entered the area where the next cargo pod was being filled. She had a backpack full of food and water and when no one was looking, entered the pod and dug her way down to the bottom then made herself small, so as not to alert the others that there was something extra in the capsule. Within several hours the capsule was closed and sealed. It had air in it as it was also used to transport people to the station. The capsule was weighed, adjustments made to the rocket software for the mass, then it was hoisted atop a large rocket and sent into space. The process took only a few days. She was cramped but managed to stay comfortable. Once the capsule was in orbit, the weightlessness loosened up the other cargo and gave her more room. Within 18 hours the capsule was captured and docked onto the starship. As it rested there waiting for someone to unload it, she opened the hatch, got out and closed it again. Then she made her way into the ship's warehouse to hide again. Within a few days, she knew enough about the activities on board to come out and pretend to be a legitimate crew member. She fit in perfectly and any issues with paperwork missing was quickly resolved, both by her and the people who enjoyed working with her. The other astronauts recognized her talents early and put her to work on sensitive sub systems and life- support equipment. She became indispensable. She smiled at one point, when she was alone, when she realized her plan had worked.

Within a month of very active work, they were ready to depart. They all took thier places on board and felt the acceleration of the main engines as they broke orbit and departed for the constellation Cygnus.

Her last act before she strapped herself in was to send a message to her flight instructor, anonymously of course, it read:

"I landed just fine."

PERFECT MEMORY

"Time moves in one direction,
memory in another." - *William Gibson*

It had snowed for two weeks straight. Nens had used the lousy weather to spend extra time in the lab. She and her staff were close to a breakthrough on their research into memory. Her staff usually went home around 5:00 which then gave her quality time without interruption when she stayed late. Her mind could concentrate on the tasks much more efficiently. The down side of course was a lack of social life as the routine turned into weekend work as well as many late nights. What generally was left after a long day was a bit of decompression time followed by sleep. This wasn't a matter of being obsessive, as most people thought, it was more a matter of seeing the goal get closer and more and more in focus. It drove her hard but progress was being made.

What they were working on was a modified cell that would work on the telomere components of the DNA strands to improve the function of nerve cells in the human brain. The research was funded by a pharmaceutical firm that was interested in producing drugs for people with memory disabilities like Alzheimers. The company had set a series of goals and had funded the researchers based on milestones. So there was constant pressure: realize progress or loose your paycheck. It was a road to burnout, and several technicians and clinicians had left during the slog. Nens remained the leader and under the most pressure as her staff looked at her to make sure they got paid at the end of the week.

Yes, the pressure was thick in the lab, however at some point, Nens realized that not only were they making measurable progress but they had inadvertently discovered other benefits from their research. The first step was to define the problem, what area of the brain was responsible for not only retaining memory but also losing it. They had discovered that the brain was capable of retaining most if not all of its experiences under certain curious circumstances. Giambattisto Vico, an Italian philosopher, was an ordinary person until he fell off of a ladder and had a brain injury. The journals of medicine and psychology have references to people who became savants after brain injury, remembering great details including phone numbers, birth dates, history, etc. It was a window into the ultimate capability of the mind, and Nens thought this research was very important.

At some point she knew she had achieved the progress required to obtain the next level of funding and made a personal decision to go off track for a bit and explore one of their findings.

One of their discoveries was the fact that with the appropriate pharmacology the nerves could be set to retain perfect memory.

The issue was not that the memory was not there in the mind, it was that it was hard to get to. The brighter people on this planet had the ability to access more information; the less intellectually agile could not, not because they did not have the information, they just could not get to it. Nens found a series of enzymes and DNA modifications that could fix this problem.

Before she actually tried anything, she thought of the consequences and on a rare, clear day, actually left work and went to a coffee shop to consider the issue of having people with perfect memories around. Would they have problems? Especially around others who did not have the "gift?"

For answers to that, she had to meet and understand the people with the highest IQ s. She made a list of people to visit and critique. There were Nobel laureates, famous research scientists, astronomers and professors. This was the obvious list. What she was also interested in was those who chose not to pursue academic or scientific careers. She had heard of a few people who had to live outside of regular society to keep out the "noise."

Next she took a week off to visit two Nobel laureates, one in Colorado and one in Massachusetts. This would take two days, then she would find the hidden ones, the ones with social interaction issues. One of these was found in Toronto, another in a local bar.

Colorado was cold when she landed in Denver. She rented a car and made her way to the National Institute of Standards and Technology in Boulder. There she met with a specialist on superconductivity. She found him pleasant, well spoken, driven and basically balanced in his approach to those who he worked with. He had realized that he could not do all of the work himself and thus had learned to work with others.

Next came MIT, where she found a professor who was absolutely brilliant, knew it and let everyone around him know it. This was his defense mechanism, looking down on others because they were not at his level. His courses were very tough and he sought no friendships amongst his students. He was generally unavailable for staff meetings and hard to get along with.

Then to Toronto she went, meeting a savant who was in the music business. He had been a chess master at age nine in New York City, then off to MIT at age 15 for a college degree. He did not finish and was hired as a vice president of a large aerospace firm which he left after two years declaring that "they are all idiots." Next he started his own company that developed holograms with amazing properties like very deep fields of view and multiple colors. After that he wandered a bit, delving in special effects and finally music. Nens met him at his office and was instantly set off balance by his questions and movements. The first thing he did was touch her belly saying "your not pregnant." She calmed herself and once the pleasantries were complete asked a few questions. He instantly knew what she really wanted and addressed the issues directly.

"Yes, I drink a lot and do drugs, it's the only way to stop the horror of the mentally challenged."

"I see. Lots of noise?"

"Way too much noise. Also I have to be the smartest person on the block at all times. I could not do that in New York so I came here."

"I understand."

"I spend a lot of time partying, that way I can lower myself to others. I usually end of scaring them anyway and have very few friends. Is that what you wanted to hear?"

"Not exactly, I am interested in the effects of very high IQs on people and what might happen if more people were at that level."

"I read your research and that of your colleagues, you will be able to achieve your goals of perfect memory but that will be a Pandora's box of nightmares and I advise against it."

"If not me then someone will do it."

"Yes, you might not realize that many other groups are on the same trail. Mostly government labs intent on making super soldiers and the like. People are not ready for perfect people, they need the flaws to navigate their way through life. When you make your Frankensteins there will be no flaws, just egos and tension."

"Hmm, okay. As you know we are trying to help......"

"That's secondary, your real interest is making geniuses. You will alienate most of the people of the world if there are too many of us."

"I understand and I will think about your words."

"I hope so but don't think you will change, there is too much money in it."

"It's not about money, it's..."

"You have to go now, I am very busy and getting tired."

"Okay, well I appreciate your time today."

"Bye."

She had to leave quickly, as he immediately rose and showed her the door. She walked quickly down the hall and at one point looked back. He was not there-probably off doing some other genius activity.

She came home to meet the final person who purportedly was a local sage who spent most of her time in a bar. Through rumors and shady connections she found herself in a dark, semi-quiet bar actually near where she worked. She went in and, looking around could not tell who she was looking for. Asking the bartender for help, she was directed to a woman sitting in a booth, with a few empty glasses keeping her company.

"Hello, my name is Nens. I have been looking for you and was wondering if I could ask you a few questions."

"Sure, sit down."

"I am working on a new drug treatment that will help people with memory problems."

"I know," she interrupted.

"Oh? How much to you know about it?"

"Everything, even things you don't know about it."

"How could that be?"

"Most of the people who work in your company have been here, mostly Friday afternoon clubs. A few come here more often and I have heard quite a lot about your work. You are going to be successful, but there is "the law of unintended consequences" that you need to be concerned with. And I suppose that is why you are here."

"Yes, in fact that is exactly why I am here."

"Well it's going to be problematic, having so many people with superior intelligences coming out of your factory over there. This will not be a comfortable world for them. It will be frustrating more than anything."

"How do you cope?"

"Drinking helps. I sit here and listen to people repeating themselves, getting the facts wrong and generally shorting themselves out mentally. It's disheartening to see how better we could be but continually refuse to do the work."

"I understand. But now we are talking about a world of competent people."

"Competent but will they be driven? You need both to get anywhere."

"Hopefully both."

"Well it's no guarantee, there are a lot of extremely smart people eating cat food in the woods. They can't stand the stupidity coming out of the rest of society and they can't stand each other. So be careful with your witch's brew and plans to create a thousand Einsteins."

"We will be, and by the way Einstein was a pretty decent person even surrounded by incompetence."

"That's because he had several layers of protection, first from his second wife Elsa, then academics, then the government."

"Okay, so you think this is an unwise move?"

"Might be, depends on your real intensions. You are supposed to be helping Alzheimer patients and now you want to make money creating Teslas."

"Maybe that is what will happen but my goals are different than that."

"How so? Are you going to enhance yourself first?"

"That's an option."

"Well when you do, come visit and I will introduce you to my nightmare."

"I shall and by the way, it doesn't have to be a nightmare, you can contribute."

"Whenever I have done that I have found a bunch of people riding my coat tails. They are just leeches and are only interested in stealing."

"Pretty dark statement. Is there no place for your genius?"

"I'm sure there is but sometimes it's more fun to get tanked and watch the circus."

"Got it. Well thanks for your time."

"No problem."

With that she left the dark bar and made her way back to the lab to pick up where she had left off. They were happy to see her and the pace of activities started to increase with her presence.

Soon they had the proper proportions to try curbing the debilitating disease with several volunteers. She administered the doses and watched these people slowly get better or at least not get worse. Many of them had lost so much brain matter that it was too late. For those in the early stages of the malady, improvement was obvious. For her it was the signal to try some herself.

Nens did not have any symptoms as she was young and did not have a family history of the disease. She also did not want to try this experiment on anyone else.

A few months later she was again working in the lab late at night, left alone and to her own devices. It was a little after 9:00 pm which was her planned time to start the experiment. She rose, walked to the lab door and locked it. This was not necessary as the facility was guarded well and had a significant amount of surveillance equipment. She locked the door for personal reasons.

Then she went to the computer that controlled the drug mixing and dosage. Previous tests had shown that a particular combination of genetic modifying agents and neural enhancers caused brain activity and quality to grow significantly in laboratory animals. They had grown several "Algernons," but as this was not their ultimate goal it was considered just a stepping stone and marked "interesting" but nothing more.

She dialed in the percentages that had had the greatest effect and filled a syringe with the concoction.

It was 10:00 pm now as she used alcohol to clean her arm, then injected herself with the full dose.

The immediate effect was disappointing, just a slight stinging feeling then nothing. She sat there in the lab for several minutes trying to tell if her mind was changing in any way. The mouse trials had gone very quickly but her brain was significantly larger and would certainly take more time to modify. After even a few more minutes she gave up and walked back to the lab door to unlock it. Then she cleaned up any evidence of her furtive attempt at stardom and went home.

Again, later that evening she felt nothing, poured herself a glass of wine and watched a bit of TV. At the usual time, she went to bed and soon fell asleep.

At about 4:00 am she started to dream in color and without the misty realm of the unreal permeating the "story" she was watching. This time it was if she was wide awake. Although the "story" was a bit unrealistic, she could move about in it without effort, talk to people and modify the surroundings at will. This was by far the deepest dream she had ever experienced and she had the distinct feeling that she might not be able to get out of it.

As a result of her cerebral panic, she nearly jumped out of bed and took a huge gasp. She sat up and realized she was fully awake with her heart pounding. There was no other choice but to get up and try to stay awake during the day. Somehow she thought that would not be a problem. Her mind was crystal clear and remembering every detail of the dream including somehow the exact time that it started, as if she had counted the faint ticks of her bedside alarm clock.

Coffee was not necessary but she made a cup anyway to satisfy the addiction. After letting it cool substantially, she drank it in one gulp. Then she reviewed the latest news, which was only a few hours older than the last, and got ready for work. She decided to walk this morning, mainly because she realized that her mind was moving so fast that she would lose concentration on the act of driving.

The door slammed behind her as she headed for the sidewalk during the first moments of dawn.

"Today will be horrendous," she thought randomly.

After a fast paced walk, she arrived at the labs and walked up to get her badge checked.

"Didn't you just leave?"

"A big deadline today, lots of work to make it."

"Okay, don't hurt yourself," the guard said with a smile.

223

Without another word (because that would be a waste) she walked to the elevator, waited but a few seconds, and then to the stairs as the climbing would be less boring than waiting for the elevator to show up.

She found a co-worker inside just getting started.

"Hello boss," the co-worker said, "early day for you."

"Yes, and our approach to this problem is totally wrong."

"How so, it seems to be working on many of the patients."

"They need to be rebuilt, not healed."

"That's not going to be easy and out of the scope of our contract."

"I don't care, we are wasting time. I am going to order a complete revamping of our efforts, we need to start working overtime."

"Oh, my. I don't think that is going to go over well with the rest of the staff."

"Their problem, not mine."

"Okay, are you going to tell the program managers about this change?"

"No, they won't understand. I want complete secrecy and locked doors from now on."

"Okay, you got it. You must have had some interesting dreams last night."

"Indeed."

Nens walked briskly away and into her office where she started writing memos and redirecting the efforts of this lab. As the others filtered in to start work, they were greeted by several-page instructions of what tasks they needed to perform and when. The workers looked at each other and decided they had to do what the boss wanted.

Within a week, the results were in from the redirection and the new formulas and techniques tripled the yield and quality of their neural enhancing drugs.

The workers were astounded, happy and worried. They had made great leaps in a short time but their boss was scaring them at times. One commented on the situation:

"She is rarely here these days and when she is here she is manic. Talking to herself, not talking to us, running around everywhere. We're not sure what has happened to her but we suspect she might have self-medicated from a previous batch of drugs we had made. Some was missing and the security systems showed she had locked the laboratory doors the night the drugs went missing. We are concerned for her safety and her mental health."

For Nens, the reality was now very different than that the workers were observing. They bored her, most everyone bored her. She was bored with her work and lamented that it was going too slowly for her. She was interested in much more challenging occupations and ideas. She felt that her mind was going all of the time, even to great places, it was just going all of the time, and, it exhausted her. There were moments when she needed to have the voices stop in her head. She saw math, she smelled emotions, she heard the whole Earth at once. It was at times overwhelming.

At some point she needed a break and could only think of going back to the bar to see the person who had found a way, albeit a bad way, to cope.

She went over one night and this time the bar was more active. She found her friend sitting at the same table as before, this time with others.

The woman saw Nens approach and sensing the situation, asked her booth mates to allow her to talk to her new friend privately.

"That was quick, must have been a strong dose."

"My brain hurts, I think I am in trouble."

"Welcome to my world, honey....waitress please bring two martinis for my friend, put it on my tab."

"Thank you, will that help?"

"The first two prepare you for the journey, the next two get you started, the last two quiet the noise. Then we will see what's really going on."

The drinks showed up and Nens gulped the first in one motion. She started to drink the second but before she did she looked up at her friend.

"This world is filled with idiots."

"From end to end. You have some options here: you can take advantage of them or take care of them. Which way do you want to go?"

"If I take advantage of them I can have anything I want. If I help them that is not guaranteed and it will be a frustrating journey."

"Turns out both options are frustrating. Turns out that you can have what you want by playing the stock market. If you help them you will discover the fundamental laws that govern our existence, many of which are good. You will find that benevolence is the only thing that guarantees success as a species."

"I have a lot to learn then. My past has been mostly academic and technical. The philosophic attributes you speak of are not something I have been interested in."

"But those attributes have followed us since the first written words. Things will make more sense if you listen to the elders. In most cases, people are smarter than they talk and you of all people understand the relationship of memory and access to memory. That is why the Socratic method is so useful. Waitress, another round please."

"Wow, these drinks are powerful, my mind is slogging through mud right now."

"Good, enjoy the ride. But remember this is only the first step. Next you have to learn how to regulate. Remember the Greek maxim, "Nothing in excess.""

"Yeah, sure, okay."

"Then when you are ready you will be given a chance to make the final step."

"And that is?"

"Sobriety."

"I don't like it already. And, and, who are you to talk? You hang out in bar all of the time drinking."

"A drink, not many. And most days I don't drink at all."

"You should be a monk, ha!"

"I have been, and in a way I am. Even though I remember everything that has ever happened to me, I still like the company of others. As I mentioned before, there are quite a few people out there who don't cope and live in the woods. Eventually they go crazy. Staying here in this booth allows me to hang on to reality a little bit longer."

"A bar? Reality? Ha!"

"I hear about everything here, about people's lives, about their work, I know scientists like you and cops, I know drug dealers and school teachers. They all have something bubbling up in their mind that they need to deal with. Below that are other bubbles-sometimes they need to deal with those instead but they wait until damage is done. From this mess of humanity that you see here comes advancements. If there is a tragedy people vote together, if there is a new gadget they talk about it and do the same. If nothing is going on they revert to their normal quarrelsome state. I don't have to watch the news, I get the highlights every night."

"Yeah, sure you do. Over and over. It would drive me nuts. Where's that drink?"

"On its way, Einstein. And by the way, your co-workers are really worried about you."

"Who cares?"

"They do, and you should. They work for you out of respect and therefore share your dreams. You need to understand that, or they will leave you."

"Yeah? Well that's okay cause we found the cure."

"No you didn't."

"Yeah I did, I'm living proof, my IQ is near 300."

"It's unstable."

"No it's not.....where's that drink?"

"Yes it is and you and all of your patients are going to crash."

This news caused Nens to sober up a bit. She looked incredulous.

"How do you know that?"

"Because you used an accelerant that the antibodies in your system will break down eventually, hopefully you will revert to your former self."

"Former self? I do not want that!"

"I'm not so sure."

"No, you're not telling me the truth, you're not a biochemist, how could you know about all of this stuff?"

"I listen."

"Yeah, well it's a waste of time."

"Maybe so. And if you don't mind I have some others waiting to talk to me."

"Yeah, well, good luck with the peasants. I'll think about you when I am getting my Nobel prize."

Nens smiled and stumbled up into a walking stance then motioned goodbye to everyone and left the bar. She mumbled to herself on the way home enjoying the fact that she could think about most any subject and know quite a lot about it. She smiled at her talent as she fumbled her keys to get into her apartment. Then she shut the door, shook off her shoes and made her way to the sofa where she passed out.

That night her dreams were muddled and difficult. They passed without resolution.

She awoke to a splitting headache and a tortured soul. She remembered most of the conversation the night before and above all, the searing look in the woman's eyes when she was warning her.

Nens showered and went to work late.

She entered the laboratory and all eyes went to her with questions. Nens could sense this and simply said:

"I need some coffee and then I will be out to talk to all of you."

The workers, in silence, went back to their chores.

About 20 minutes later, Nens reemerged and pulled up a chair in the middle of the group of workers.

"What accelerant did we use on batch 486?"

After a bit of research,

"The standard type 4."

"Is it susceptible to human anti-bodies?"

"Probably."

Nens stopped for a second to reflect on the consequences of the decision to move forward with the development of the drug.

"I made a mistake."

"We know."

"How would you know? How would you know that I injected myself with the 486?"

"The logs do not match the remaining amount of 486 and security has been asking questions."

"Oh my. Well I am sorry for this, it was selfish on my part to try some."

"That's okay, we understand. You have been under a lot of pressure to move this research forward. We knew you were going to try this."

"How could you have known? I told no one."

"Wanda knew."

"Who's Wanda?"

"The owner of Persephone's bar down the street."

"How could she possibly know what I was going to do? She does not work here."

"She knows everything. And she has done some very good things for our neighborhood."

"What do you know about her?"

"Well, she has been here for a very long time, my grandparents knew her. She used to be married to someone named Pluto or Plato or something. People think that she is very old or maybe from another star system. Just conjecture of course and she laughs about that if you bring it up to her. She has always owned that bar and made a lot of money somehow. She is our best kept secret which is the way she wants it. We think she is extremely smart but does not show it unless it's really necessary. She remembers everything and can predict people's actions well in advance. Her bar is named after the Goddess of vegetation, who was abducted by Pluto and taken to the underworld. She tries to escape every Spring-that is why we see the plants growing out of the ground. But she is drawn back every Fall and that is why we see the vegetation retreat into the ground before Winter."

"Interesting story. But I don't believe in voodoo or astrology."

"She is neither, she is well beyond any of that. We think she is here to guide us."

"We will see."

"We already have."

NOTABLE QUOTES

"It's not so much the twilight as it is the dusk. Born at midnight, mature at dawn, settled at dusk."

"The only way to experience the future is to invent it."

"We are capable of more than we can imagine, although venturing to the stars is next for mankind, one wonders what will occur after that."

"Kindness is the language which the deaf can hear and the blind can see." - Mark Twain

"Life is like a coin. You can spend it any way you wish, but you can only spend it once." - Lillian Dickson

ABOUT THE AUTHOR

Kevin Shoemaker was born in New York City in April of 1954. A son of an actress and musician-turned-professor, he has lived in several states and has been educated in the fields of philosophy, radio astronomy and antenna design. He has authored several technical papers in astronomy and has many patents in the fields of aviation, antenna design and meteorology. In addition, he is an avid pilot and boat owner and holds several certificates for operating airplanes, helicopters, performing flight instruction and is a licensed Captain in the Merchant Marines. Currently he works as an antenna and radar designer near Cape Canaveral, Florida. Mr. Shoemaker is a father of one daughter and one son and lives in Indian Harbour Beach.

Comments? e-mail: Shoemakerlabs@gmail.com

Other books by the author:

Mars Life

Practical Antenna Design

The Voyages of Gaea

Sunrise Descending

Life in the Universe and Where to Find It

Views from the Balcony